A STRANGE AFFLICTION

By
Marie Piper

For Grandma Mary-

Who taught me how to witch for water.

Editor: Megan Bacalao Virkler

Cover and graphic design by:

Aleisha Knight Evans

Table of contents

Chapter One

June 1692

Only a half-moon peeked through scattered clouds. The darkness made for good cover as Hannah Hibbard crossed the waist-high grass that filled the field between her home and the edge of the forest.

She dared not light her candle. Only when she was far enough from the village would that be safe. At night in the vast Massachusetts darkness, a flame would only serve as a beacon drawing notice to her presence. Being noticed shone its own light on habits that could be twisted into a good claim that a plain woman was a witch.

Witches went to the gallows in Salem Village now. That was a fate Hannah to avoid. After all, she *was* a witch.

Not the broom-riding sort of witch from lore and fables who cursed her neighbors. She could not conjure storms or dry up a milk cow. Any of her neighbors would attest that Hannah was a good and kind Puritan woman who had no dealings with the Devil. Yet, she did know plants and the earth better than most, and used them both to help and to heal. There was a time when her knowledge had been no great secret to those who knew her, but those days were gone now.

Hannah had curtailed her weekly practice of venturing to the forest, hence why she was out to gather plants in the hours before dawn on that mid-June morning. Namely, she needed some blackberry leaves for Goody Thorne who had trouble with her bowels, and jumpseed for the terrible rasp in Oliver Reed's lungs if she could find it. Anything else she found interesting on the visit to the woods could be used in a variety of teas and poultices. There'd never been a time in her life when Hannah's pockets hadn't been stuffed with plants and roots, her fingernails dark with the dirt of her explorations.

Reaching the edge of the forest, Hannah stepped in among the hickory, oak, and hemlock, and let down the hood of her cloak.

Breathe.

How she loved the woods.

The sort of magic Hannah used, though Hannah would never have called it magick, was as old as the earth itself, as old as mothers and grandmothers in kitchens and in front of fires since the pagans had thought the stars themselves to be gods and feared them, and since the witch hunters had ravaged Europe and her own grandmother and mother had crossed the wild Atlantic to find freedom only to land among the Puritans. They had joined the faith, committed themselves to God, and then Hannah's mother had married a Puritan man and hidden in plain sight as easily as putting on a new dress.

Many things were different in America, her father had always said.

Her mother would always reply that some things, like witches, were the same.

Salem Village was certainly not the same as it had been in Hannah's childhood. Since February, when Betty Parris and Abigail Williams and the other girls had started naming women as witches, it seemed the whole world had flipped upside down. People Hannah knew well had been accused, jailed, questioned and questioned again and again about nefarious acts that good Puritans would never consider and should never hear tell of. Citizens who had been outgoing and friendly now kept to their houses. Everyone looked sideways at everyone.

Going unnoticed was of utmost importance for Hannah. A quiet and admittedly strange widow who was known to work with plants would be too easy a target.

No one was to be trusted.

The madness was an infection. Anyone might be infected, and infections spread.

The furor had grown so great that now the new Governor of the Massachusetts Bay Colony had finally appointed a court and named judges to oversee the trials that had begun so as to bring some order to the community.

The whole affair was wild madness. Hannah stomped ahead deeper into the forest, angry. She kicked a branch that was in her way. If she could have been certain there would be opportunities in the coming weeks, she would not have even ventured this trip into the woods tonight.

A representative from the Governor was coming to Salem, one of a number of men who'd come to see the events over the tumultuous past five months, as if wealth and business experience could salvage order from the chaos. The Reverend Samuel Parris had decided this representative would board at Hannah's home.

While a bit flattered that the Reverend found her good enough to represent the town, she was also irritated. With a man in her home, her comings and goings would be noticed. How was she to gather herbs and mix remedies without attracting his attention? And what sort of man would he be? All the men who had come to see about things so far had been pompous know-it-alls. Unfortunately, the man was likely to be the observant kind, so if she was to have any time to do her work, she should probably gather a few things for a sleeping draught.

Crack.

Hannah went still.

But it was only wind, or maybe an animal. Nothing of consequence.

If she was going to be home before sunrise, she needed to move faster. Keeping eye and ear open for other noises or movement, she walked quickly toward a clear patch where she had found the thin tendrils of jumpseed the summer before. Reaching the familiar patch of ferns, she dropped to the ground and lit her white candle with a match. Under the little light it cast, Hannah pulled a small knife from her sleeve and bent to the plants.

In amongst the strings of jumpseed, mint and dandelions stood lively as if welcoming her back to the woods. She snipped some and slid them into the pocket of her apron with the rest. With its crisp aroma, mint could ease an unruly stomach and help with sleep. The choppy leaves of lovely yellow dandelion were good for skin rashes and the flower also made a very pleasant tea.

Hannah scooted to another plant and felt something other than dirt beneath her fingers.

Raising it to her face, she saw black muck on her hand.

"Wet ash," she muttered aloud.

The moon and her candle cast just enough light to show where the ground was blackened. A few remnants of charred wood lay scattered a few feet away.

There had been a fire here.

It was unlikely the Penobscot would come this close to town, so this was not an Indian fire. Besides, there had been little sign of any of the tribes since the massacre in York, Maine on Candlemas, though tales of that horrible slaughter had kept the colonists awake, listening for any creak of a footstep outside their door for months. But no one ever told horror stories of the French and white men who had ridden with the Penobscot on their rampage. War was an ugly, hideous business no matter who was participating. It was never easy to forget that King William's War was happening fifty miles from where Hannah knelt.

No, this fire was done by someone local. A piece of firewood nearby had clearly been split and brought to that spot.

Those foolish girls must have come here.

The remnants of the fire were not very old, for they'd had a hard rain four days past. Even now, when suspicions were high and citizens were scared, a few still came to dance. To think these few were the ones who'd first done the accusing.

Sighing, Hannah made quick work of destroying what was left of the fire. Best to leave no trace at all.

The accusations of witchcraft had started quickly and now flew fast as crows. Two young girls in the family of the Reverend Parris had started having fits and blamed it on witches, and had named the witches too. Their servant Tituba was a witch, they said. Sarah Good was a witch, and so was Sarah Osborne, for they had all cast spells on sweet little Betty Parris. More accusations came, and more and more. Now the accusers were not just children, but grown men and women as well.

A few words from some little girls sent all Salem into hysterics.

Even now, the infection still spread.

A lump formed in Hannah's throat when she thought of all the women, and a few men, who languished in jails in Salem and Boston and even up in Ipswitch, awaiting their trials. So many were people she had known for years and had never imagined could ever consort with devils and demons. Could you ever truly know someone? For God to have shown so many church-going people to be dark-hearted, something must have gone terribly wrong in what had always seemed a peaceful village.

Raised a member of the Puritan faith, Hannah knew what to believe. Her father had taught her what was true and what was not. The Reverend said witches were real, so certainly they were real. Certainly, most everyone accused was in consort with the Devil. For how could it be otherwise? It was not the Puritan way to lie. The Reverend said it was so, and Hannah did believe him. At least, she did her best to.

Then, Rebecca Nurse had been accused. It was she who kept Hannah awake.

Rebecca was the most pious and Godly woman Hannah had ever known. Yet, she too was now awaiting trial because two men from the Putnam family had accused her. Seventy-one years old, almost deaf, infirmed, and Rebecca had been sitting in prison for weeks. How could any court find her to be a witch? How could Reverend Parris or anyone else think it so? If a full covenanted member of the church like Rebecca could be a wife of the Devil, what good was anyone?

Hannah felt a tear run down her cheek when she realized that once again she had questioned God's will. She wiped it away and into the ash, ashamed of her weakness of faith.

The weaknesses came more and more often these days.

She had ever so many questions. For all her father's teaching and how Hannah had always obeyed and done what she should, she was still her mother's daughter. Her mother had been beautiful, but wild somehow, like a flower among a field of rye.

Hannah tried to remember to trust in God. For that was the Puritan way.

Salem Village was in trouble because the Devil had come to town. The victims were authentic and plentiful, girls screaming at devils in the rafters of the church, testimonials of hauntings and afflictions, a slew of people charged with that most heinous of crimes.

If Rebecca Nurse had signed her name in the Book of the Devil, then she deserved the hanging that would come for her. They all did. It was an ugly thought.

But Hannah simply could not believe Rebecca would do such a thing.

Sighing, Hannah leaned against a tree and cast her eyes to the moon.

Perhaps if Hannah had believed more in God and less in the moon, she would not be a widow. Perhaps her lack of belief combined with a collective lack of belief was the reason for all of the trouble. Maybe if they all believed more and worked harder none of this would be happening

Hannah wiped her nose on her sleeve and sucked in the warm night air.

Summer in Salem had always been a happy time, an easy time when what could be grown came to harvest, and the angry beating of the winter that had just passed and would come again in a heartbeat slipped from the minds of the citizens for a while. There was music in summer. There were gatherings. The previous winter had been harder than any Hannah could remember so she meant to savor the summer warmth while it lasted.

Clearing her thoughts, she listened only to the trees in the wind.

Something still chilled her.

This place was something more than just woods.

No wonder the girls had come here.

Those were dangerous thoughts better saved for another time and place.

Quickly, Hannah returned to collecting herbs. All she could do was pray, work harder, and keep herself and those closest to her safe. She filled her apron pockets with plants until they were stuffed, put up her hood, and left the woods.

Hannah would go back to her home and her hearth and hide herself away.

Nicholas Cleary hated Salem Town upon first sight.

It wasn't the gray sky or the stink of fish from port city fishermen that first stirred his distaste. He'd come to town by hopping aboard a supply ship, and his nose had adjusted to the smell of the sea hours earlier.

No. It was the women. As he moved from the docks to the main street of the city, each one he passed looked upon him as if he were the plague. His rumpled clothes and mussed black hair from the nap he had taken on the bow of the boat didn't make a good first impression.

Perhaps he should take a drink of rum from his flask. Drinking was fun.

Salem was a Puritan town. From what Nicholas knew of Puritans, they did not look kindly on fun. That had always seemed strange, as the first Puritan ship, the *Arabella*, had carried three times as much beer as water and ten thousand gallons of wine on the journey to the New World from Holland.

Nicholas liked drinking rum, even though he could not drink it without thinking of the poor souls in Barbados and on the other Caribbean islands who slaved over the sugarcane it took to make the stuff. Barrels of molasses traveled even on the ship he'd arrived on, bound to become more rum.

It would not do to be seen drinking in public.

So Nicholas straightened his spectacles, resisted the calling of his flask, and asked a man for directions. He soon wound up handing a man a coin and loading his small trunk on the back of a wagon bound the five miles west from the port city of Salem Town to the more rural farm community of Salem Village

Legs hanging off the back of the wagon, Nicholas pulled out his paper and pencil.

Nicholas had been sent to Salem Village as an observer to report the happenings of the newly appointed Court of Oyer and Terminer back to the equally newly appointed Governor William Phips. He was to notice anything unusual, although how he was supposed to pick one unusual thing from a whole series of unusual things, Nicholas didn't know. The more he'd heard about Salem, the whole business seemed unusual. People in Boston had many theories as to why it was happening, but none of those theories explained all the people imprisoned and the stories that trickled to the city.

Regardless of reasons, Nicholas planned to solve it all and return to Boston in triumph. Then he would embark on a long and prosperous career of writing about religious hypocrisy and the wonders and blessings of being, in essence, a heathen, while drinking and carousing as he pleased.

That, after all, was the secret of life. Men were fallible, even those garbed in the Lord's words, and it was best to find pleasure when and where you could, while trying to help others along the way.

Before the glorious future of his dreams came to pass, though, Nicholas would need to survive Salem Village.

As the wagon moved away from Salem Town, buildings became farm fields. The clothing of those he passed became simpler, less colorful. The Village was poorer than the Town, but the two communities fed each other and needed each other.

The wagon stopped in the center of crossed dirt roads among the high fields.

Nicholas jumped off and pulled his trunk with him.

"Do you be Mr. Cleary?" An old man with a head of shockingly white hair stood frowning at him. The man stood in the middle of the road, but Nicholas had not noticed him before and had no idea where he'd come from.

"I am he."

The old man stuck out a worn hand in greeting. "I am Anson Bittner. Expected you yesterday."

"I was waylaid in my departure." It was not a lie. A ravishing yellow-haired beauty had indeed waylaid him. Seeing the hour grow late as they had lounged in bed, the time of his departure had been pushed off. Nicholas accepted Anson's hand and shook it warmly.

Anson nodded. "Then it is God's will you made it at all."

"God's will and my Captain's skill," Nicholas retorted while knowing it was not the answer he should have given. He needed to remember to hold his tongue in Salem Village. They were Puritans, and the purest of their religion. By just his one response, Anson could mark him as an enemy and his entire reason for coming would be doomed.

Yet, Anson Bittner did not frown. In fact, Nicholas would have sworn he saw the old man bite back a smile. "Is that trunk all you have?"

"I find it easier to keep an eye on my things if I travel light."

"Well, you won't have to worry much about thieves around here." Anson picked up the hefty box and set it in his wheelbarrow as if it weighed nothing, then picked up the handles of the wheelbarrow to push. For an older man, he was remarkably strong. Likely the result of a lifetime of nothing but work.

"I can push," Nicholas offered, embarrassed to have the older man doing the work.

"You are a guest," Anson said. "The Hibbard place is a bit of a walk. Reverend says you're to stay with the widow while you're here. She's a God-fearing woman, and has room since the death of her husband three years past."

"Goody," Nicholas muttered ironically to himself. "Has Mrs. Hibbard been made aware of my coming?"

"Aye. She is being paid to keep you, too."

Staying with an old widow did not seem like any sort of fun, but Nicholas could not argue. Perhaps the compensation would be enough to keep the widow out of his affairs. He was lucky to be in Salem at all. Not many disgraced writers were granted a second chance, especially not after being caught in a dalliance with a prominent businessman's daughter as well as caught writing salacious pamphlets. Nicholas needed to remember to bite his tongue and be grateful to Governor Phips.

Perhaps, as long as Nicholas was quiet, the widow Hibbard would not mind his habit of staying up late to read and write and drink until the sun rose each day. Or perhaps she would expect him to chop wood and do other household tasks.

As he followed Anson past houses that grew farther and farther apart, he saw all ages of men and boys hard at work chopping, sawing, and building. Nicholas wondered if he'd be so bored within a day he would be asking to chop wood.

Anson turned down one road cut from high wheat, and the houses that had dotted the landscape grew even farther apart. The old man walked quickly, not at all winded. "Whose land is this?"

"This here? Why, this land belongs to John Proctor."

"No, I mean which Indians lived here before you all came?"

"Oh," Anson tilted his head. "I remember the Naumkeag people from when I was a boy. That means fishing place, I think." After a pause, he continued, "So you've come to write about the trials?"

"Aye. What do you make of them?"

"Interviewing me already?"

"Might as well get started." Nicholas pulled paper and pencil from his coat.

Anson wrinkled his brow as if considering his words. "'Tis hard to know what to think. God willing, the truth will become clear to us all and no one need suffer much longer. Are you of the faith, sir?"

"No I am not."

"Any faith?"

"None in particular."

"Didn't think so," Anson remarked.

It was exactly the sort of answer Nicholas dreaded hearing. As if he should just trust that God would take care of the madness. Over a dozen people sat in jail already. It seemed to Nicholas that God was either not interested, or worse, that he was in over his head.

Soon a house came into view over the crest of a hill. It was no different than any other house they'd passed, made of dark wood with a pointed roof with a barn set a short distance away. Yet this house appeared to be surrounded by a lush green garden in the middle of the wide open field. "There's the Hibbard place now," Anson said. "Charles Hibbard farmed rye, but my sons and I tend to that now. That there is Hannah's garden. She works with all sorts of plants. You'll see." He called up to the garden. "Hannah!"

The garden was fenced in by wood slats, but the plants grew wild over the sides. A few vines even crawled up the side of the house. Bright flowers of pink and yellow bloomed near the windows. At the sound of Anson's voice, someone rose and cupped a hand to the sun before waving back.

Nicholas stopped walking. "Is that her?"

"That be Hannah."

"Mercy," Nicholas muttered. Even from a distance, he saw clearly that the widow Hibbard was not the old crone he'd expected, but a tall woman of maybe thirty with lean limbs and a pleasant shape. She came from the garden wiping her hands on her apron and met them at the end of her property. As she approached, Nicholas noticed copper hair beneath her white coif, and a stern face formed of fine features.

This beauty was his hostess? Perhaps Salem wouldn't be so terrible after all.

"How are you today, Anson? Once again I have made too much bread, and I hope you will take it off my hands."

"I am well. And I will always take the bread you make." Anson swatted Nicholas. "You will be sorry to leave it behind when you return to Boston. This is Hannah Hibbard."

Hannah Hibbard looked Nicholas over as if he was a less than prize hog. "So you are Mr. Cleary."

19

"Nicholas Cleary." He bowed slightly.

"I was told I am to house and feed you," she replied in a curt voice. "I welcome you to my home." Folding her hands together over the skirt of her russet dress, she looked over his clothing. "My daughter Sally will tend to your washing while you are here."

"What has happened to Mariah?" Anson asked.

"She left," Hannah replied. "Scared off."

"Scared off?"

As if he were a fool, Hannah blinked at him. "The witches, Mr. Cleary. The same reason you have come."

Back in Boston, Nicholas considered himself good with the ladies. He'd had affections and dalliances as any man of thirty-five should, more than his share if could tell the truth freely. The women he was drawn to fluttered and flitted and giggled and gossiped. Wickedly clever and accomplished, they wore feathers and floof and would never have been seen with dirt beneath their fingernails like this woman.

Hannah Hibbard had dirt on her hands and would not faint away at his charms. In fact, she appeared to already dislike him. Perhaps he'd dressed too finely, or perhaps she could read the stamp of *sinner* on his face. However she saw through him to his very soul, Nicholas thought the stiff-backed widow was the sort of person he would face on his judgment day.

"Trunk to the back room?" Anson asked.

"Thank you." She spoke softer to Anson and it was good to hear she was not cold to everyone, only him. Anson headed to the house with the cart, and Nicholas let Hannah follow before moving behind her. He straightened his hair and tried to remember all his best manners.

The main room of the house was filled with a large wooden table and six chairs. One whole wall was an impressive hearth and cooking area surrounded by pots and pans and drying herbs. A ladder led to an upstairs loft. Nicholas breathed in the scent of wood and smoke and something glorious beneath it.

"What is that wonderful smell?"

"Cloves."

An orange cat scooted past Nicholas so fast he nearly tripped. "You have a cat."

The widow stood a few feet from him, hands still folded tightly. "That is Carrot. It is more like he has me. Your room is through there." She acknowledged the room with only a bob of her head. "You will be given breakfast and our midday meal."

"That will be more than enough," Nicholas replied. He peeked into his bedroom and saw a bed, desk and chair, and candle, and a window that looked out toward the forest that encircled the fields. Anson put his trunk at the foot of the bed and Nicholas set down his satchel and removed his coat. He slid his trunk against the wall under the window and tried not to think about the additional difficulty of an attractive female hostess.

He had not come to Salem for women, of all things.

"Here are two loaves," Hannah was handing Anson bread in the main room when Nicholas rejoined them. "Have you any word of Rebecca?"

"Nay," Anson answered. "But I've heard that Martha has taken sick."

"Oh dear."

"Rebecca Nurse?" Nicholas had finally heard something of interest. "Are you speaking of Rebecca Nurse?"

Both Hannah and Anson shot him solemn looks. "What do you know of Rebecca?"

"The accused are infamous. Everyone in Boston knows their names."

He had not thought it was possible for the widow Hibbard to have more distaste for him. He had been wrong. "They are not infamous to us. They are our friends and family. You would do well to remember that," she said sharply.

"Of course." Like he'd been slapped awake, he knew she was right. This place was the belly of the beast. Everyone in town would know someone, likely many someones, afflicted or accused. Though Nicholas thought it all a wretched mess, he could still feel sympathy for the people left behind to hold the pieces together when members of their family had been snatched away. There was a time to make smart comments, and a time to be quiet and a time to tread carefully.

"I'll be taking my leave," Anson said. "Thank you for the bread, Hannah. Mr. Cleary, should you need anything my home is the one we just passed."

"I thank you for your help, Mr. Bittner."

"Anson."

"Call me Nicholas."

With a wink, the old man left and turned to haul his cart down the road.

Nicholas was left alone with the scowling widow Hibbard. Despite the warmth in the room from the summer day and the fireplace, he felt an undeniable chill. To ease her, he moved toward the table and admired the skill with which it had been built. Turning to his hostess, he indicated Anson Bittner. "He has the strength of a man of twenty."

"Anson had done the work of four men long as I have known him. When my husband passed, he took to me and my daughter like a father would." She was watching Anson go away from the house, and clasped hands had not eased.

"I fear I have offended you. Such was not my intention."

Hannah turned to face him. "Are you a man of God, Mr. Cleary?"

He would get that question a lot in the coming days. "I am a believer in something greater than ourselves, though I confess to sometimes doubting our Lord believes in me."

"You did not answer my question."

"If you mean do I subscribe to all these demons and specters," he waved a finger in the air, "the answer is no. I have been sent here by Governor Phips for a month, maybe less, to document what is happening and has happened. What I believe or do not believe does not matter."

"Do you think it could be resolved in a month's time?" There was disbelief in her question.

"I am hopeful."

"The Governor was here weeks ago but has not returned since. I thought he did not particularly care what happened here."

"He may not care much," Nicholas admitted. "But the hanging of Englishmen and women has alarmed the King. Therefore, it alarms Governor Phips."

"But it is the church that has sanctioned the hangings."

"Perhaps that is what has concerned him most of all." Easing into the topic, having heard her mention the name, he added. "In truth, it is Rebecca Nurse that has raised questions and brought me to this place. Her family has been quite persistent that she is innocent of all charges." He waited for the widow's response. If she was as close to one of the accused as he suspected she was, then he knew exactly where to begin his work.

"Rebecca is as Godly a woman as walks," Hannah said.

She frowned deeply. He had hit a nerve. "You know her?"

"Everyone knows Rebecca. She delivered many of the children of this town."

"Then why has she, an old and infirmed woman, been sitting in a dank cell for months under accusation of witchcraft?"

Hannah had reached the fire and poked at the embers with, Nicholas thought, a bit too much enthusiasm. Her brow was furrowed and her jaw tight. "I do not know, Mr. Cleary. 'Tis a question that robs me of sleep."

The woman was troubled. He would not have guessed her a woman who could be troubled. She looked like a woman who could handle just about anything.

"Something is rotten in Salem Village, Mrs. Hibbard." Nicholas sat in chair at the table and removed his glasses to wipe them clean. "That's taken from a line in Hamlet, a play by William Shakespeare if you don't know it. I have been sent to see if I can sniff out why that is. I could greatly use your assistance, and will not name you in any writings I do or any meetings I hold."

With her back to him, he could not read her expression. But she stood unmoving for far too long for his suggestion not to have struck something in her. If he could crack the hard widow, perhaps he could make even the slightest crack in what was going on in Salem.

"Perhaps if you spent more time reading your Bible and less time reading dramatics, you'd better understand the trouble here," she practically spat before storming out of the house back into her garden.

Chapter Two

Hannah spent the afternoon pulling weeds from her garden.

It was not that her boarder was a man of no faith, a big city skeptic who quoted dramatics and had come to Salem Village with presumptions about the backwoods nature and beliefs of Puritans that infuriated Hannah. None of that was new.

The infuriating thing was how handsome he was. Devastatingly so. She had nearly fallen over upon first laying eyes on Mr. Cleary.

A homely man in her home would have been easy to ignore as he walked around her kitchen and poked at the hearth to keep the fire glowing. Having a large, strong-built ruddy man with a crooked smile suddenly around was almost too much to bear. Just because she was a widow did not mean she was unable to notice the thickness of the wild black hair he absent-mindedly ran his hand through, or the way his strong thighs filled his breeches, or…

"Stop this," she whispered to herself.

Not two hours after he arrived, she had to sit with him at her table for the mid-day meal, the largest meal in a Puritan day. Thankfully, he had already spread papers over one end of her table and was deep in his ink and words while she turned risen dough onto a floured block and worked it into a braided loaf for the following day.

He removed his spectacles. He had lovely dark eyes.

God grant me strength, she thought to the rafters.

She added some rosemary to the bread for luck.

Like an answered prayer, Sally bounded into the quiet room. Twelve, and suddenly so much taller than she'd been just the year before, her white blonde curls fell loose from her coif as she raced into the house. Sally never walked when she could run. The very force of her nearly sent the papers Mr. Cleary was scribbling on right off the table.

"Mother, you will never believe what Mercy said! She heard from Lucas that Caleb told him that he overheard Philip Noyes saying that Sarah Osborne had once…" Sally had not even noticed the visitor, but he had looked up with great interest.

"Sally!" Hannah barked louder than she had intended. Puritan girls were to be quiet and go unnoticed.

"I am sorry, Mother," Sally whispered. She finally saw the man in her dining room and her eyes grew wide as attempted to smooth the wild vines of her hair.

Hannah stepped to her daughter. "This is Mr. Cleary. He is the boarder I mentioned. He will be staying with us for a while." Sally's eyes lit up. Always curious, always questioning. "Now help me with the stew."

Sally gave a quiet curtsey and wordlessly rushed to the hearth to help Hannah pour hot stew into brown bowls. Venison stew with potatoes and carrots and a few herbs from Hannah's bottles, the dish took two days to make and had been one her husband had always enjoyed. Served with rye bread and fresh butter and cider, the meal would do much toward filling the stranger's belly until he was too tired to be awake. He would go to his room and into a deep slumber. Then the moon would rise and Hannah would be able to attend to her work again.

"Thank you," Mr. Cleary said when Sally delivered his food. Hannah and Sally sat at their usual seats at one end, leaving the head seat left vacant. Mr. Cleary was down at the other end, separated by at least two yards from them. "This smells delicious. Again, Mrs. Hibbard, I am grateful to you for lodging me."

"It is no trouble," she replied. "The Reverend suggested I would be best, as we have room." *I had no choice in the matter*, she hoped he understood.

"Reverend Samuel Parris?" Mr. Cleary asked.

"He is our minister," Hannah nodded. She would allow no crack in which to slip into a conversation about the hysteria. "How was your afternoon?" she asked her daughter.

"Oh, lovely. Mary and I worked on our tapestry and then we…"

But Mr. Cleary didn't need a cracked door to sneak in. He pushed it wide open and interrupted, "Mary Walcott?"

Sally looked at him with confusion. "No. There are a great many Marys around here, Mr. Cleary. But I know Mary Walcott."

"Tell me, Sally, do you know many of the afflicted girls?"

Sally eagerly nodded and answered, "Salem Village isn't a large place. We know most everybody. Especially those our age."

If Mr. Cleary had not yet heard the tale of how Mary Walcott's aunt had taught Tituba how

31

to bake a witch cake of someone's urine, rye, and ashes, and feed it to a dog to determine if that person was a witch, he would not hear it at Hannah's table. Hannah set her spoon down hard on the table. "Mr. Cleary, I cannot allow conversations about such matters to take place in my house."

"Whyever not?"

The stupid man did not see the danger that swam in the air. The ghosts and specters formed of nothing that brought people to their deaths. To him, the hysteria was something to study, an oddity to poke at. For the residents of Salem Village, it was life or death. Yet if Hannah spoke those words, it would terrify Sally, and she had done so much over the past months to save the girl from the worst of it all and to keep from thinking there was any danger to their house. "We have not yet said a prayer," she countered.

Mr. Cleary did not take his eyes from hers. "My apologies."

"Sally."

Sally bent her head and recited the prayer perfectly. Hannah barely heard. She found herself peeking. Mr. Cleary did not bend his head or close his eyes, instead choosing to look out the window, but at least he did not interrupt.

"Amen," Sally concluded.

"Amen," Hannah repeated.

Mr. Cleary said nothing. The silence was oppressive, overwhelming. They each took a piece of bread and began to eat. Hannah blew on her spoon before taking a second bite of the savory meat and vegetables. She again missed her late husband and how he had never pushed on any topic, preferring to sit in silence and listen to Sally's chattering or to read to them from the pages of his Bible.

This next month was certain to be agony.

Sally never could bear silence. "Mr. Cleary, where do you come from?"

"Boston, now. But I spent many years in Pennsylvania."

"Were you born there?"

He shook his head and did not speak until he had swallowed his stew. "I was born in London. I came over here as a boy."

"Do your parents live?"

"They died in London. I came over as an apprentice to a newspaperman."

The girl's eyes grew wide. "I cannot imagine what cities like Boston and London look like."

"Boston is only fifteen miles from here. Have you never been?" Sally shook her head. Mr. Cleary appeared genuinely troubled by that. "Well, cities look much the same as here, save for taller buildings and far more people. And the people in those cities dress differently."

"Are they not Puritans?"

"No, they are not," Hannah replied, hoping Sally would read the order to hush in her expression.

Mr. Cleary huffed. "I thought judgment was to be left to higher powers."

"I do not think at all about those city people," Hannah answered. "There is no time to think about them. Our lives are not spent in dalliance. We work hard here, all day long, and keep to ourselves." She saw the way he chuckled before biting into the bread. "Is something amusing, Mr. Cleary?"

"When I mentioned my assignment here, I was told that Salem Village is the most quarrelsome village in the whole of Massachusetts. So far, I'd have to agree."

"I would hasten to say you have only been in Salem Village a few hours. You have not seen a fraction of how quarrelsome we can be."

At her words, he almost choked on his stew.

Sally stood quickly, having cleaned her bowl. "Mother, may I be excused to my lessons?"

"You may," Hannah said. Sally took her dishes to the wash basin and all but rushed up the ladder to her loft. Perhaps Hannah saw Mr. Cleary watch Sally out the corner of her eye, but had she imagined that? The man wanted to ask questions, and she would have to warn Sally to keep her mouth shut. A young girl was easy prey for a man good with words.

Mr. Cleary wasted no time. "Is Sally friends with the afflicted girls?"

"I don't want her dragged into this. You are a guest in my home and I welcome you, but I cannot allow these questions of either Sally or myself." Hannah kept her voice low as she rose from her chair. She could no longer sit at a table with him.

"I do apologize, Mrs. Hibbard."

Hannah returned to the hearth and dealt with the dishes while he finished his stew and bread. He brought her his bowl and she took it without a word, then he returned to the table, picked up his messy papers and inkwell, and retired to his room.

Only when the door closed behind him did Hannah feel at ease.

The midsummer sun slowly went down, necessitating the lighting of a candle at Hannah's work table to aid her in seeing the bundles of herbs she was gathering and hanging to dry. The smells of the mint and sage and the feel of the leaves under her fingers brought her peace and allowed her mind to wander.

Nature was far less complicated than human matters.

Perhaps she should run away to live in the woods.

She laughed to herself and pressed leaves to her nose to inhale the scent.

As it grew darker, the low light from under Mr. Cleary's door continued. He needed to sleep so she could sleep. After selecting leaves from her pouches and drying bundles, she heated water and took a cup of tea to his door.

The door opened at her light knock.

Hannah regretted the tea immediately. Before her stood the stranger in a loose white shirt unbuttoned far enough for her to see the strength of his chest and the light hair that crossed it. Hannah had been prepared for anything except the surge of heat racing across her skin from head to toe. "I brought you this."

"What is it?"

"A tea to help you sleep."

"What is in it?"

"Oleander. Blackberry leaves."

Nicholas Cleary raised one eyebrow. "Isn't oleander poisonous?"

"If you use it incorrectly."

"Are you trying to poison me?"

"If I was, you'd never know."

He smiled. Oh, but his smile was appealing. He accepted the tea from her hands, and as their fingers brushed Hannah sucked in a quick breath and then hoped he hadn't heard it.

"May I ask you a question, Mrs. Hibbard?"

"Does my permission actually matter?"

"Are you a witch?"

She looked him directly in the eyes, embarrassed at his ignorance. "Be careful what you say around here. That sort of a question gets women hanged these days." She turned to go, but his next words stopped her from dismissing him.

"Again, I apologize. I did not mean to offend or worry my hostess. You have my word I will not ask Sally questions, and I will do my best not to trouble you with them as well." When she looked back at his face, she saw a surprising sincerity there. "I am an impulsive man, Mrs. Hibbard. I will try to aim my questions elsewhere."

"That is all I ask."

His shoulders moved in a shrug. "For what it's worth, I don't believe in witches."

She scoffed. "Then what do you think is happening here?"

He seemed to brace himself. "I believe all this madness comes down to the greed of one man. Your Reverend Parris. He is said to be overbearing, and too fond of gold candlesticks."

"We all know the history," Hannah bristled. "Salem Village has had a hard time of finding someone to lead our services. Parris is fourth in a line of men who could not handle the position in recent years, and his time here has not been free of disagreements."

"Is that so?"

"A dispute over his pay lead to the village ceasing payment of any kind back in October. He was not even brought firewood for the winter."

"He can't have been happy about that."

"Whether the Reverend is happy matters not. I do not appreciate the insinuation that there is nothing wrong here save for one man. As for your calling it madness, go and ask Bridget Bishop if it's no more than madness."

Mr. Cleary nodded. "Where might I find Bridget Bishop?"

Hannah growled her answer. "I don't know where her body is now. They hanged her on the tenth of this month. She was the first, and she isn't likely to be the last."

Instead of shocking him, she had only piqued his curiosity. "See now. That's something. Was Mrs. Bishop a witch?"

"The esteemed Court said so."

Mr. Cleary seemed honestly surprised at her answer. "If it is not madness, or the influence of one man, what do you attribute all this to?"

As if Hannah had not fallen asleep every night for months rolling that question around in her mind. Was it actually madness? A collective sickness? Poison? Treachery? Lust? There was no simple answer, no single thing that could be pointed to that explained the rot at the core of Salem Village.

Hannah gave him the best answer she had come to. "A sickness in our souls."

Without another word, Hannah returned to her fire.

If the widow Hibbard hated him, and he absolutely suspected she did, it was of little consequence. He'd be out of her home in a month or two, headed back to the comfort and ease of Boston. In the meantime, he would do what he did best, which was to question too many things and write too much about them.

Moving to lay on the small bed, Nicholas couldn't settle. He remembered the large featherbed in the fine room he rented, overflowing wine at social gatherings, and the attentions of a few pretty women. His childhood had been hard, but he had used his skills with words and a pen to make something comfortable of his life.

Sleep did not come easy despite the tea.

Nicholas woke at dawn and dressed quickly to get to the village meetinghouse first thing for the morning service.

It was time to meet the Reverend Samuel Parris.

Before leaving Boston, Nicholas had asked around about the man and had formed what he felt to be a solid impression. Parris was a Harvard-educated spoiled brat who inherited a plantation in Barbados and, after somehow managing to ruin it, taken up the faith and come to Salem Village to dupe the locals into paying him to talk at them.

Nicholas could not abide men like that. Men made of weak stuff but born into privilege who easily danced their way to positions of power they were unqualified to hold, determined to have people listen even though they had nothing real to say and nothing of assistance to offer the world. A leader of any faith should not be concerned with candlesticks and silver, but rather in helping the souls who looked to him.

It was Nicholas' plan to expose Parris as the rotten apple spoiling the bunch.

The truth seemed to stand there and stare at him. He could not fathom why others could not see it as clearly.

In the Salem Village meeting hall, citizens sat quiet as ghosts on wooden benches. Reverend Parris stood before them and spoke, his loud voice carrying over the rows of people to where Nicholas stood leaning against the back wall. The Reverend had brown hair worn to the shoulders, an almost regal bearing, and a prominent nose. Nicholas half-listened, and took the opportunity to study people who seemed interesting. Salem was not such a large village that everyone in the room did not know someone or other either accused or doing the accusing. What stories could any one of them tell? What secrets did they all keep?

Not a person among them smiled. They listened, attention rapt. There was no joy in these walls and in this worship.

Being a stranger, many pairs of eyes darted to him and away again when they saw him looking back. Nicholas had dressed down in plainer, darker clothes not unlike their own, but he knew he did not belong. So did they. He could practically smell the suspicion.

Parris droned on. Nicholas sighed and did his best to pay attention.

After the service, most people filed out the back doors but Nicholas pushed forward until he was face to face with the man he meant to uncover. "Reverend Parris?"

Parris turned to him. The man was as tall as Nicholas and met his eyes directly. He wasn't pleasant looking, but was also not ugly. His face could best be described as forgettable. "May I help you, sir?"

"I am Nicholas Cleary. Governor Phips sent me from Boston to report about the trials."

Parris sneered. "This is a matter for God, not the Governor." Of course he would say that. The man's high opinion of himself filled so much of the room Nicholas was amazed others could get even get in. "If the Governor is so concerned, could he not return himself?"

"He is occupied with the French and the Indians to the north. And he has Stoughton and the others keeping him updated." Nicholas pulled paper from his coat, ready to begin his questioning. "Since the appointment of the Court of Oyer and Terminer…"

"Are you a Godly man?" Parris folded his arms. Somehow, despite their being the same height, he managed to look down on Nicholas.

"I am not."

The scorn in Parris' eyes did not seem like something a holy man should be able to show. Parris picked up a book and did not look back as he strode toward the door of the hall, calling back over his shoulder though Nicholas followed him. "I have souls in need of saving, Mr…what was your name?"

"Cleary. Nicholas Cleary."

"Mr. Cleary, please stay out of my way while you are in town." With that and nothing more, the Reverend Parris moved to exit the hall and walked away. He moved down the street, nodding to all who recognized and greeted him as if he were a

Lord making his rounds rather than the self-effacing head of a humble congregation.

"Well la-di-da," Nicholas spoke aloud.

A chuckle came in response and Nicholas looked over to see a man outside the church. He was dressed in the same clergy garb as Parris, but smaller and leaner, with light brown hair and eyes that smiled. A peace lingered around the man. If Salem Village was a hurricane, this man was a peaceful breeze.

Nicholas liked him immediately. "Is he always like that?"

The man gave a wry smile. "He did not want you to come."

Something we have in common, Nicholas thought. "Oh, I do not doubt that. Who are you, friend?"

The man stepped to Nicholas. "I am Reverend John Hale of Beverly. If Parris is unwilling to speak with you, perhaps I can assist."

"But this is a matter for God, not a representative from the Governor," Nicholas tried Parris' words against the new reverend to see what the reaction would be. Beverly had once been part of Salem but had been broken off as its own town to the east, a natural boarder being formed by the Wooleston river.

Hale held his hands up. "Our souls answer to God, but our physical forms are held just as accountable by the government. In truth, I am glad to welcome you. More hands make less work, I've always felt."

"That is why the Court of Oyer and Terminer was appointed."

"Oyer and Terminer. What does that mean?"

"To hear and determine," Nicholas answered.

Hale looked after Parris. "There are men who are happiest when they answer to no one, who hear and determine what they desire to. Perhaps you've been sent here by someone other than the Governor."

He likely meant God, but Nicholas chose to ignore that. "Spurred by the insistence of the Nurse family, I have come to write a report for the Governor as to the events here. Yet so far both the Reverend and my hostess, the widow Hibbard, will not speak to me about it."

"Hannah Hibbard is a respectable woman," Hale explained. "And these are not respectable things for her to discuss. She is protecting herself and her daughter. I'm sure you can understand that."

Nicholas felt guilted. "Do you know her?"

"I knew her husband. Charles Hibbard was as honorable a man as ever lived. Now, I am happy to answer any questions you may have. But you must walk with me, Mr. Cleary. I find walking a pleasant way to pass the time."

As Hale walked slowly, he spoke. "The Puritan faith was born of the desire of a group of Protestants to reform the loose ways of the Church of England. We believe God formed a covenant with us. As such, we are charged to set a good example. The first Puritans here came to this new world with the intention of creating a haven, a City on a Hill as it were."

Nicholas knew all that. "You believe that one's eternal soul is judged from birth."

"Yes. And so we live our lives as well as we can."

"But if you are judged at birth, why not live your life as wildly as you want? Why not drink and carouse?"

"But we do not want to do that."

Nicholas had never understood that. "No matter their God, people want things. They desire things. Money, the flesh of another. No one is a saint."

"We aspire to be worldly saints, Mr. Cleary."

"I wish you the best of luck with that." Even the most pious of men could not resist temptation. Nicholas had seen it all too many times. How many holy men had been caught in entanglements? How many church-going political men had mistresses and secret children?

Still, Nicholas scribbled down all the things Hale said. The man did not storm away from him or even register any irritation. He was calm and collected, and spoke so well and honestly Nicholas was grateful for their encounter. Following along, scribbling in his notebook, Nicholas took to asking Hale everything he could about Puritan ways and life, and what it was that might separate Beverly and the other parts of the colony from Salem. There had been accusations of witchcraft in the other colonies, but not to the quantity of this cluster. Here was a man of some authority who might know why.

"What makes Salem Village so different?"

"I cannot say."

"How many are currently in jail?"

Hale stopped, for they had reached the edge of the water. "Last I knew, sixty-two people were in custody at the end of May."

"Sixty- two!" Nicholas dropped his pencil. "They cannot all be witches."

"The accusations against each of them appear credible. More trials will begin in the next few days."

It was madness, an absolute madness. "What do you know of Rebecca Nurse?"

Hale shook his head. "Now, she is a woman I would never think could be corrupted by such evil. She is a full covenanted member of the church here, same as Martha Corey. Thirty-nine members of the community signed a petition in Rebecca's favor. She goes to trial on the thirtieth."

"Her lawyer will undoubtedly present that petition to the Court."

"The accused are not allowed lawyers."

Ridiculous! How could a trial happen without lawyers? Many of these farmers could barely read to sign the documents court required. Nicholas ran a hand through his hair and rubbed his face, walking in a circle. "And what if her accuser is lying?"

"Ann Putnam accused her, and she is an innocent child."

Nicholas felt like throwing his notebook in the water. These backwoods ways would get more women killed same as Bridget Bishop. "Children are not all innocent, Reverend." He'd lived in

Boston long enough to know that. Circumstances could make even the sweetest souls go bad.

"How do we tell those who aren't, Mr. Cleary?"

It was a fair question, and rendered Nicholas silent.

Reverend Hale bent down and picked up Nicholas' pencil and handed it back to him. "Let me tell you a story about one of our afflicted girls, Mercy Lewis. Mercy was born in Maine. Her entire family—mother, father, aunts, uncles, everyone she had in the world—were killed by the Wabanaki up there in the Candlemas Massacre."

"It wasn't only the Wabananki. The French attacked, too." More than a hundred people had died in a foolish squabble, yet only the native people seemed to be blamed. The hypocrisy of it all infuriated Nicholas.

Hale nodded. "Mercy was sent here and into the service of the Putnam family. She suffers from understandable nightmares and nerves. And yet through it all, she is as obedient a child as I have ever known. If she, who has seen so much evil with her own eyes, can remain good at heart, then would it not be safe to say that children are closer to purity than anyone else?"

"Are all the afflicted girls as good as Mercy Lewis?"

"They are all from good families. Betty Parris is the Reverend's daughter and Abigail Williams his niece. Little Ann Junior is the daughter of the Putnam family, who wield considerable influence around here. Mercy Lewis lives with the Putnam family, and Mary Walcott is their niece. These are not bad children."

"You are convinced it is possession and witches."

"I see no other reasoning for things being as they are."

"Why here? Why so much more in Salem Village than anywhere else?" He needed Hale to point at Parris.

Instead, Hale looked to the blue of the sky. "George Burroughs was Reverend here for a short time ten or so years ago. He was then the Reverend up in York in Maine where Mercy Lewis' family was killed. He said that these troubles were God showing his displeasure with this land, and I find some truth in those words. Perhaps these troubles are a trial for us all."

"This Burroughs seems a wise man. Taking the new land by force and blood from people who have been here since time began seems like something that would anger a just God."

Hale held up his palms as if to say he did not disagree.

Nicholas put his pencil against the paper. "Where might I find this Reverend Mister Burroughs?"

"If you want to speak with him, I believe he's in Ipswitch jail."

"Is anyone in this horrible place not in jail?" Nicholas sighed loud and hard, squeezing his pencil so hard it should have broken. Hale stayed silent while Nicholas controlled himself. "Can you at least point me to the site of the hangings?"

"It's that way, past John Proctor's land and Read's Hill."

Nicholas closed his eyes. "I suppose this John Proctor is in jail."

Hale nodded. "Aye, and his wife too. Accused by Mary Warren, their servant. Elizabeth Proctor is with child as well."

Nicholas felt like hitting something. "Thank you, Reverend."

"Find me again if you wish to ask more questions. I am in town to assist as I'm needed and will always find time to council." Hale was leading to something with his careful words, and Nicholas recognized it.

"Will it be my soul you attempt to save next? You will not be the first man of the faith to attempt it."

Reverend Hale simply smiled and folded his arms across his chest. "If you feel you need to be saved, I will do my best to help you."

There were many things Nicholas needed, but salvation was not among them. Even if the offer came from one of the kindest men he had ever encountered.

Pushed onward, needing to be alone with his thoughts, Nicholas left the Reverend there by the water and headed for the gallows.

Chapter Three

Hannah's habit of waking early had begun when she had become a mother. Even as a baby, Sally could not sleep past first light. Now, as she grew into womanhood, the girl had begun to sleep a bit later, but after so many years of waking early Hannah enjoyed her time alone before the day began.

When she emerged from her sleeping quarters beside the hearth, she was surprised to find that Mr. Cleary was already out of the house. She had imagined him lounging until midday and living slovenly when at his own home, yet when she went into his room to make his bed it was already properly made. Carrot had made himself comfortable on the quilt.

Mr. Cleary did not seem like the type of man to make his bed. Perhaps he had done it to keep from angering her.

She needed to not think about him or his bed.

A neat stack of papers and a quill and pen laid on the small table, next to a copy of *Memorable Providences*, a pamphlet by the minister Cotton Mather. Hannah had heard tell of the pamphlet. It detailed an earlier witchcraft case in Boston. Goody Glover had worked in the Godwin household, before the children of the family had begun to have fits and accused her of witchcraft. Irish, and Catholic, she had hanged for witchcraft five years earlier, but word of the tale had spread even to Salem Village.

The cat meowed and stretched.

"You hush," Hannah pointed a finger at it. "I'm only looking."

After blowing the previous night's embers back into a true fire, she began the work of her day. Bread need to be baked, eggs had to be collected and chickens always needed wrangling. In addition, there was a garden to tend, and meals to be made. After setting the first bread to bake, Hannah took a cedar stick and carried it around the rooms, waving the clearing smoke into every corner and sending a few extra puffs into the room her boarder used.

Sally came down the ladder and fumbled to braid her long hair up around her face the way she liked. Not for vanity, but practicality. A girl could not run with her hair in her face all the time.

"Let me," Hannah said, and moved behind her daughter. There was so little time left before Sally went from a girl child to a woman and no longer needed her mother. The feel of the silken hair in Hannah's fingers was familiar, and she wanted to hold the memory of the wee wiggly child and those early days.

"Is Mr. Cleary here?"

"He has gone out."

"Already?"

"Apparently."

Sally turned her head. "Why aren't we to speak with him?"

"Face forward." Hannah took a deep breath. "Salem Village is not his concern."

"Perhaps he is trying to help."

"Perhaps." Perhaps he was a grand know-it-all who was nosing where he didn't belong.

"Perhaps we could use his help."

Avoiding the urge to scoff, Hannah could have smiled at the innocence of the child. Sally had no experience with arrogant men who assumed they knew everything and that everyone else was an ignorant babe. "Yes, perhaps he is." Hannah tied off one braid and turned Sally to face her. "But it is not our concern, his work. He is here to document what is happening. Blessedly we are no part of that."

Sally's eyes looked straight into her mother's. "But these are our friends, Mother. I'm very

55

troubled. Aren't you?" Sally was right. Hannah had again lost sleep over the imprisonment of women she knew and admired. Martha Corey. Rebecca Nurse…. Sally continued, "Do you think my real mother might have been a witch, and that's why she left me—she was hanged?"

Though Hannah had never denied the child was not hers by birth—not to the child and not to anyone else—every mention of it stung. To her very marrow, Hannah felt Sally was her child. They never spoke of it except among themselves. Those who knew Hannah well knew the child had not been born of her body, but that was one nice thing about living on the outskirts of a small village. People tended to mind their own business. "What would make you say such a thing?" Sally did not answer, and Hannah rushed to reassure. "I think perhaps your mother was a fairy, but you are no spawn of a witch."

"Abigail says there are fairies in the woods." Sally whispered it dreamily.

At the mention of Abigail Williams, Hannah felt her heart race. Sally did not need to go chasing fairies and wind up neck deep in this madness. Hannah dropped to a knee and took the girl's hands in hers. "Sally, hear my words. For the time being, you stay clear of Abigail and Betty and all those girls. I don't want you spun into all of this."

"But what if the Devil picks me?"

Oh, but the fear on Sally's face made Hannah want to scream. How to explain the wickedness of men and the enormity of witchcraft to someone who still thought the stars to be diamonds in the sky sent by God for decoration? "Sally…"

"It could happen, Mother."

Hannah put a hand on Sally's cheek and felt the smooth skin of youth. "The Devil will have to go through me first, love."

After a breakfast of brown bread and butter and coffee, both women went out the door their separate directions. Sally was helping a group of younger girls with a quilt, while Hannah aimed for town. With so many of Salem Village's women in jail, many children and men had been left without the women who did so much of the daily work in their homes. Hannah would deliver fresh bread to several, and teas and poultices to a few others while she picked up some smoked fish in the village.

A man's voice called to her the moment she reached the edge of the village. "Hannah!"

It was Harmon Webb, and she put on a smile as if the sight of him didn't cause her to groan inwardly. "The day shines brighter upon the sight of you, Hannah," he drawled.

"Good morning, Mr. Webb."

"Harmon," he corrected.

There was nothing physically wrong with Harmon Webb. He was tall and lean, with the fairest of hair and sharp features that many women considered attractive. No, the thing Hannah disliked about him lay down in his soul, in the way the back of her neck prickled at the sight of him. "Mr. Webb, unfortunately I cannot stay and talk. I must…"

"I'll walk with you."

He walked too closely for Hannah's comfort, chatting at her in the way that men could when they didn't really want to hear a woman's thoughts but rather wanted someone to talk at and wanted for people to see them with a woman to stake their claim. He spoke of land deeds and market prices and Hannah counted the shutters on the houses and buildings they passed to make the time go by, for she had always found him desperately boring.

Harmon stopped walking. "Have you considered my proposal?"

Not a month earlier, he had proposed marriage. Hannah swallowed. "I have already told you, I am not interested in remarrying."

He scoffed. "What woman isn't interested in remarrying? To be a wife is the highest honor."

She bit back bile that he thought she should be honored. "I have been married once, Mr. Webb. Bless my late husband's kind and humble heart, it was enough for me." She longed yet again for Charles to be there, to not only be a friend and helpmate, but also for the natural protection a husband offered a wife merely by existing as a looming specter. It was unfair but undeniable that a man's claim on a woman made many men steer clear.

Harmon took a step closer to Hannah. "You cannot manage your land and home alone."

She forced herself not to take a step back and away. "I manage my land and home every day, and I have Sally so I am never alone."

"Your dress is frayed, Hannah."

"I am humbled, Mr. Webb."

Sensing he would not be victorious with kindness, Harmon's face twisted with a coldness that almost made her shiver despite the warm day. "It's not right for a woman to be alone. People will think you a thornback."

Better a thornback than a carpet to be walked on, she thought. "Again, I am not alone."

"I hear you've a boarder."

"Aye. Nicholas Cleary of Boston."

Harmon's eyes narrowed more. "I would urge you to reconsider my proposal, Hannah."

"I would waste no more of your time on me, Mr. Webb. Good day." Before he could argue more, as she knew he would, Hannah swept away into a shop to purchase her fish.

Their encounters were increasing, and a knot was beginning to form in her gut when she came to town knowing she would have to resist his pushing. Why could he not hear her words and accept her decision? Though she had walked away from Webb with confidence, by the time she concluded her purchases in town and arrived at the Andrews' door to deliver a remedy for aching bones to James Andrews, Hannah was rattled and had to take a deep breath to steady herself.

"Ah, Hannah," James Andrews greeted her with a warm voice but barely a smile. He was a mostly stoic man on the best of days, but was as troubled as anyone else lately. Every house near his had been affected by the trials. A number of his neighbors were currently in jail for accusations. Hannah had often brought remedies to the Corey's, but Giles and Martha were both imprisoned now, though the thought of either of them being witches was near ridiculous. Cantankerous and argumentative, certainly, but witches?

"For your pain," she said, and offered him a pouch of herbs. "Drink it in tea and it should help, God willing. There is ground willow bark in it."

"Can I offer you a rest?"

Hannah saw that the sky had grown cloudier. "No, thank you. I'll be heading home. Bread won't bake itself."

"Did you hear Martha has taken sick?"

"I will pray for her."

"Hear you've got yourself a boarder."

It was likely everyone knew by now. "Aye."

"Where from?"

"Boston." James scoffed.

Hannah chuckled. "Word travels quickly."

"Aye. Saw him not a half hour ago headed over to the gallows. He looked a state. If you need any assistance with that one, you let me know."

What on earth would make Nicholas go to that horrible place? Hannah thanked James for his offer and returned to the road.

One way down the road led her home. The other right to the gallows, where apparently Mr. Cleary was making a spectacle of himself.

There were still enough hours in the day to give him a lecture about not being conspicuous and still be home in time to finish her tasks.

Cursing the goodness of her heart, Hannah headed to the gallows.

As he went down the written list of names of the accused a clerk to Judge Stoughton had given him after he'd sat in a pew and refused to leave, Nicholas walked from the village in the direction Hale had pointed to the gallows where the hangings had and would continue to take place.

Sarah Osborne, Sarah Good, Tituba, Martha Corey...

Rebecca Nurse, Sarah Cloyce, Mary Esty...

The list was far too long. Truly, he had come to Salem in ignorance of the width and depth of it all. Mostly grown women, and all in jail because of no more than accusations. Governor Phips had appointed a court to oversee the trials, but they had brought no reason to the proceedings, instead basing the accuracy of accusations off an English statute that provided no concrete evidence. As if it all was not absurd enough, the Governor had allowed spectral evidence to be admitted against the advice of the area's most influential ministers and popular opinion. Now it was only the word of a group of girls against all reason and logic. By the example that had been set, Nicholas could point at someone on the street and scream "Witch!" and they'd be hanged in a fortnight.

The corruption and evil of man was nothing new to Nicholas. Though he found it all terrible and absurd, nothing hit him. Nothing truly rattled him and gave him true shivers until he reached one particular name on the long list of accused witches currently in jail.

Dorothy Good. Age 4.

"My God," he spoke to the air. "What have they done?"

A four-year-old girl was in jail for witchcraft.

Nicholas stopped walking when he felt a chill cover his skin. He had reached the ledge. It did not appear anything but an ordinary spot, a bit of raised ground topped with trees and made of rock. A wooden platform extended over the spot, far enough off the ground for an execution. Nicholas was grateful to find the area empty of people. From this point, he could see the great Massachusetts wilderness as well as the chimneys and smoke from Salem Village.

Down below the ledge was a pit of sorts. Disturbed earth.

A body had been buried there.

This was the heart of the matter. Bodies and earth. Nicholas stepped to that place and sucked in a breath. He did not move again for a very long time. Until that very moment it had seemed a foolish story told by someone else.

A bit of dirt and a four-year-old girl had struck him deep and fast.

Crouching, he touched the dirt. "Ah, Mrs. Bishop, whatever did you do to get here?"

"She wore a red bodice and cursed at her husband." Nicholas knew it was the widow without even turning around. She stood closer to him than he expected, with a basket over her arm and a dark expression. "She stayed there for several days before she was cut down. Apologies if I have disturbed you."

"It is not you that disturb me."

"This is not a good place, Mr. Cleary. Not a place to linger. Are you alright?"

It must have been the water coming from his eyes that gave her cause to ask. Nicholas imagined he looked ridiculous. He wiped his eyes and adjusted his coat and hair as he rose to his feet. "Must be the northern air. Too pure for my comfort."

"There is nothing wrong with crying."

He closed his eyes. "I only this day learned about Dorothy Good."

It was a moment before the widow spoke. "I often think about her. Her mother is Sarah Good, of course. When Sarah was jailed, she was with a child as well. She has since lost that child. I cannot imagine the ordeal. Now both of them may wind up here." She looked up at the trees that hung overhead, where witches had and would hang. "That is what I do not want to happen to Sally, nor to myself."

What a strange thing to say. "Who would accuse you?"

"Anyone can be accused. Know that."

Nicholas nodded. He did. "You are a strong woman, Mrs. Hibbard. Or—Goody Hibbard?"

"I am no one's wife anymore."

"Reverend Hale mentioned your husband. He said he was an admirable man."

"That he was. Charles and I had many good years, God be thanked."

Nicholas turned and looked back in the direction of Salem Village. He'd come to solve a mystery, and he had only taken one step up a long ladder toward answers. Hale had been somewhat helpful, but he could not expect the Reverend of a nearby town to know everything. A quiet widow who watched those around her would likely know more than most. "Might I implore you to help me, Mrs. Hibbard? Might I beg enough to have you answer the questions I came here with, which are expanding ten-fold every minute?"

She looked hard at him. Nicholas felt as if she could see through his skin to his bones. It was a look not of friendship or appreciation. His heart sank.

His hostess turned to go.

"Walk home with me and tell me about yourself," Hannah said. "I will admit I do not entirely trust your motives, but I will hear you. At the end of your tale, perhaps I will change my mind."

"Change your mind to think *me* an admirable man?"

"Best not to get ahead of yourself."

There was humor in her answer, and Nicholas could have fainted. The smallest of smiles actually played at one corner of her mouth. In regular times, he would have pointed it out and used it to flirt with her. But these were not regular times and no matter how lovely she was when she smiled, she was not his purpose here. Certainly he would also face her wrath if he tried.

They began to walk, side-by-side several feet apart.

"What can I tell you?" Nicholas fell into step with her. "I was a boy in England. I had no family but I always liked words so I was apprenticed to a newspaperman and came over here under his tutelage." As he always did when recalling his life story, he left out the orphanage and the hunger, the bigger and older boys who beat him for his smart mouth.

"Where did you land?"

"Pennsylvania. I was there for several years before I moved on to Boston to write for myself. I began at a newspaper, but it turns out I like money and the comforts it provides so I embarked on a different career."

"Working for politicians."

"And businessmen and bankers. In truth, I wrote what men paid me to write. One merchant hates another? Give me coin and suddenly the man will find himself holding a pamphlet about the filthiness in his factory."

The words did not cause any change in the widow's expression. "What I don't understand is why you care about Salem Village? Are we merely another pamphlet to you?"

"My purpose here is more than that, Mrs. Hibbard."

"Then what?" She stopped walking. "A salacious novel? God forbid, a play?"

"My reasons are my own."

Hannah closed on him like a door, and began to again walk away. He saw his hope of her insight fading, and the confession burst from him. "My name is, at present, not a respected one." That gave her pause. "I wrote pieces arguing for the abolition of slavery. I spent time in Pennsylvania with the Quakers and it was there my eyes were opened to the horror of the practice. Whatever a man's skin color, he should not be treated like cattle against his will. If one indentures himself, that is one thing, but to steal a man or a child from his homeland…"

"Of course, but I don't see what this has to do with the here and now."

"Powerful men who profit off bad systems do not like hearing criticism."

"I imagine they hear a great deal of it. If it bothers them, perhaps they should rethink their business."

"They especially do not like hearing that criticism from a man who has been sneaking around with one of their daughters."

Hannah studied his face. "Ah."

"Ah, indeed."

"So Salem Village is to be your redemption for your supposed crime?"

Nicholas felt ashamed of himself. "I may have come here for selfish reasons, but I hope to leave here having accomplished something good. Something helpful."

"For yourself or for us?"

There was a straight to the heart question. "It is easy to sit at a desk and read about people and witches and Reverends and think you have the answers. It is another thing entirely to be here among the same people, to see their faces and hear them speak. I came here confident I had all the answers, and it has not been one day and it strikes me that I do not even know the right questions."

"And so?"

"So I will look closer."

For over a mile, there was only silence between them. Nicholas felt certain she would ask him to leave her home.

When they arrived at the very spot where Nicholas had stood with Anson and first laid eyes on the Hibbard place, Hannah stopped. Sally was working in the garden, pulling carrots from the ground and putting them into a basket. She was singing a sweet song though the words were indecipherable from that distance.

Hannah spoke quietly, "Tomorrow night after Sally has gone to bed I will speak with you." Nicholas gasped aloud and she rushed to add, "I do not know that my answers will help, Mr. Cleary."

"They will be more helpful than you know. And I will compensate you." He had coin for that specific purpose.

"I do not need your money, Mr. Cleary." That was a lie. The Hibbards were not rich. They farmed a poor piece of land and both Hannah and Sally's dresses were patched more than the other women he'd seen around the village.

"Perhaps not, but if you do not take the coin I will have to pay Parris, and I would rather bite off my own hand than do that." The widow's mouth curled into a smile, and with it a bit of brightness lit her pretty eyes. Her eyes were the color of tea with just a drop of milk added. "Honestly, you have given me hope in the darkness, Mrs. Hibbard. I hope you know that."

Hannah shook her head. Probably she thought he was mad.

"Tomorrow then," Nicholas said.

"Tomorrow." The widow walked away as if nothing important had happened.

Chapter Four

M r. Cleary stuck to his room most of the next day. Hannah heard his pacing steps, and the sound of paper crumpling. Though he did leave the house for a while in the afternoon, she did not know where he went. Not that it was any of her concern.

When the sun began down and Sally had gone up to her reading and bed, Mr. Cleary settled at the table. Snapping his fingers and whistling, he appeared to bubble over with anticipation. As the day went on, she had half-hoped he would forget her promise to speak with him, but clearly there was no hope of that. It took only a moment for him to remove his jacket and pick up his pen.

"What is it you want of me?" Hannah reached for her mending for a task to focus on. She could not help feeling that speaking with him was akin to walking on ice. Every word would have to be measured carefully lest she crack something and fall into danger.

Mr. Cleary cast an intense gaze at her. "I want to know what you think and what you have observed. As you know, I am a stranger here. Puritan ways and the people involved in these events don't mean the same to me as they do to you. And Parris will not speak with me."

The thought of the Reverend even looking twice at this stranger made Hannah smile. "Of course not, you're a heretic."

"And a libertine, yes, yes, so I've been told." He brushed away the comment with a wave of his hand. The hint of a smile on his face caused his eyes to crinkle at the edges. This was a man who had laughed many times in his life. This was a man who was no stranger to joy, to pleasure.

Feeling her cheeks warm, Hannah nodded. "Where should I begin?"

"Bridget Bishop, I imagine. She was the first, yes?"

"The first hanged, but not the first charged."

"And what do you make of it? Reverend Hale says that Bridget never stepped foot in Salem Village."

Hannah would be as honest as she could. "That is true. She ran an inn in Salem Town. I did not know her personally, but I have gathered no one who knew her was terribly surprised she was named a witch. Witch accusations are not unfamiliar to us, as they are not unfamiliar to you. There have been witches here and there since before settlers came to this land and before that

73

back in England. The accusations here began in February spread quickly, when more and more were named."

"Who was named first?"

"The first three woman accused were Sarah Good, Sarah Osborne, and Tituba."

"Are they respectable women, or are they, like Bridget Bishop, outsiders?"

"The two Sarahs and Tituba are, indeed, considered to be strange women. But it did not take long before respected women like Elizabeth Proctor, Martha Corey, and Rebecca were named. Martha Corey's husband Giles even spoke against her, which I never expected."

"And Dorothy Good is Sarah's daughter."

Hannah stopped stitching. "Sarah Good's accusation was not surprising. Anyone would think her a witch just by looking at her. That Dorothy was also accused may be our collective shame." She looked down to her hands. She had to believe God had a plan for the little girl on the other side of this cruelty. What could months in a dank prison do to a little girl?

There came a creak as Mr. Cleary moved his chair closer to the table. "The first women named, Sarah Good, Sarah Osborne, the rebellious Goody Bishop, and Parris' slave woman Tituba.

Are they merely difficult and strange women, or are they actually witches?" Hannah knew that God alone held the answer to that. Many of the women named did not attend church and certainly lived outside the example the Puritan faith meant them to follow. Seeing she did not have an answer to give him, Mr. Cleary continued. "Do you believe Tituba to be a witch?"

The Parris' slave woman stood out from the rest of the accused for several reasons. "I admit to ignorance about her people and their beliefs and customs. I don't know that anyone truly knows where she came from. Some say she is from Africa, others from Barbados or South America. Wherever she is from, I do not think her a malicious woman. She always spoke kindly and I and many others believe she truly loves the Parris children."

The man across the table raised one eyebrow at Hannah. "What aren't you saying? Tituba confessed fully to witchcraft, after all."

Hannah sighed. "I believe, and many others believe, that she confessed because she was beaten by Reverend Parris." He frowned, and darkness came over his face. Hannah tried to explain better. "By confessing, Tituba saved her own life. She may sit in jail for a long time, but she

75

will not hang. Only those who do not or will not confess will be hanged. A few have confessed to save themselves. Deliverance and Abigail Hobbs are mother and daughter, and they confessed for that reason, it is said."

"Perhaps the Hobbs women and Tituba are the smartest of all." Mr. Cleary scribbled some hasty notes, likely about Parris whom she already knew he did not care for. As if he could not speak of Tituba anymore, he swallowed. "Tell me more about Sarah Good."

"Her accusation was not hard to understand. She is a poor beggar prone to muttering things that could be construed as curses."

"Were they curses?"

"I couldn't say."

"And Sarah Osborn? Did she not die in jail in May awaiting some sort of justice?"

"Poor Sarah Osborn had been ill and had not been able to attend church for some three years before her accusation." The woman had died in prison, and it was too terrible to think of.

Mr. Cleary removed his spectacles and set them on the table to rub his eyes. "The Putnam family comes up often in these accusations. Something like half of the accused people have a charge by a Putnam or two against them. I've heard they bear considerable influence in town. I've also been told that Ann Putnam and Sarah Osborn were all but declared enemies."

"Aye."

"Is it possible that beneath the root of these accusations there's something far more…bureaucratic?"

"Mr. Cleary!"

He thrust a stack of papers at her. "Are you saying all these people *are* actually witches, then?"

Hannah's hand beneath her stitching curled into a fist. How could he expect her to respond with answers she had spent months trying to find for herself to no avail?

He tried another line of questioning. "Do you believe in witches, Mrs. Hibbard?"

That she could answer. "Witches exist. My Reverend says they are so, and he speaks the word of God. I do not know what evil has taken hold here, and I may not understand all the ways of the world, but I believe the accused women to be as it is said."

At her words, he sat back in his chair and fixed upon her the most irritating smirk she had ever seen on a man's face. "Riddle me this, Mrs. Hibbard. Could all of this not be, now hear me out, no more than perhaps a convenient way for a

77

selfish child to harm someone they did not like? A child who means to do well, perhaps being influenced by her father? Perhaps a family or two could easily rid themselves of problems and complications with just the word of a child."

It was Betty Parris he meant, and his intention was to place at blame on Reverend Parris. The first night he had arrived at her home, he had said as much. Until that moment, Hannah had not truly seen the depth to which he thought he had everything resolved. Mr. Cleary's ideas had totally removed the role of faith from the situation. "We are God's children. We do not lie."

"Children are children, Mrs. Hibbard." It took all of Hannah's willpower not to snatch the pen from his hand and throw it out the window as he scribbled with an arrogant smirk. "Children tell tales. Children are malleable."

The very nerve of him. When she could no longer focus on the tiny stitches, Hannah rose and went to her counter to pull risen dough from a bowl and began working it.

The girls might be sick, or caught up in a strange madness, but they were not simply lying because someone told them to. It would go against everything they had been raised to believe.

Probably three minutes passed before Mr. Cleary spoke again. It felt like three years. When he spoke again, it was in a kinder tone. "Would you tell me about Rebecca Nurse? When was she named?"

Hannah paused her kneading. "In March."

"And by whom?"

Hannah closed her eyes. "Ann Putnam."

"The Putnams had disputes with the Nurse family, yes?" Again Hannah did not answer. The answer was yes, that the feud between the Putnams and the Porters over who owned which land had gone on for generations.

"Tell me about Sarah Cloyce, Rebecca's sister. I have heard a wild story."

"There was nothing wild in it. Rebecca had only just been accused and the Reverend announced John: chapter six, verse seventy."

"You will pardon me for my ignorance…"

"Have I not chosen you twelve, and one is a devil."

"What happened next?"

"Sarah got up from her seat and walked out of the meetinghouse. The door slammed behind her. I witnessed it with mine own eyes."

"Is that unusual?"

Hannah set down the bread. "It is unheard of."

"I think I would like her." Mr. Cleary rose from his chair and began to pace, staring at papers he carried in his hand. "The Nurse family gathered a petition. Thirty-nine signatures, delivered to the Governor's desk, declaring the charges against Rebecca to be wrong. Fat lot of good it did her, though, ey? She's sitting in which jail now? Ipswitch? Boston?"

The idea of dear Rebecca in a prison cell brought the edge of tears to Hannah's eyes. "May we all have a family like the Nurses on our side in times of trouble." The petition had been so effective it had brought the Governor himself in May to observe and speak to the Reverend. Not that it resolved anything. Rebecca had not been set free. Those thirty-nine people had spoken boldly, made themselves targets, and thus far it had been for nothing. That petition had brought Mr. Cleary to her house and her to this moment of such frustration and sadness....

Hannah realized she was shaking.

"Hannah..." Suddenly, the man stood directly across the counter from her. She saw his expression, curious but something more, through her teary eyes. "Tell me. If you do not believe children are capable of lies, and yet do not believe

Rebecca Nurse is a witch, then how do you explain things?"

Hannah ceased making the bread. Even with the wood counter between them, he was so close it was improper. She could not even consider that he had used her name. "Rebecca has said herself that the Devil could have taken her form to trick others."

"Trickery," he scoffed. "And what say you to the charges she killed Rebecca Sheppard and John Fuller."

"They died of fever. Perhaps in their delirium they saw visions. Rebecca never harmed anyone in her entire life."

"You are certain."

"I would stake my life on it." Hannah would cling to that like a rope.

"And who said it was Rebecca Nurse that killed them?"

"Ann Putnam."

Blessedly, Mr. Cleary turned away and back to his papers and thoughts. As he talked, mostly to himself and muttering the seemingly endless list of names and dates and accusations, Hannah stopped listening.

As she struggled to clear her thoughts, she rolled the bread harder and pressed it more firmly.

81

If she could infuse the loaves of bread with enough love, perhaps she could do something good.

It was too late for Bridget Bishop, but it might not be too late for Martha Corey, for the Proctors, for Hannah and Sally, and most especially for Rebecca.

Watching Hannah pound the dough into a round loaf, Nicholas felt certain she could bring him to his knees if he ever truly offended her. There was trouble in her eyes, and he felt he was partly responsible. So he returned to recalling a complete timeline of the events in Salem Village thus far, and was relieved when he saw she had stopped listening to him.

The woman did not seem to realize her hypocrisy. Whereas she was completely unconcerned with some of the women accused, others consumed by the trouble concerned her greatly. She'd been moved to tears by the thought of Rebecca Nurse in jail, but no tears came for Sarah Osborne who had died in a jail.

Salem society dictated she think the way she did. The judgment was deep in her, and hard as rock.

When he could not take the way her shoulders shook another moment, he approached the counter. Impulsively, he reached out and landed his hand on hers. "Slow down, Mrs. Hibbard. The bread may not survive your wrath."

Hannah stared at his hand on hers.

Her hand was very warm. It was too forward a move.

After Nicholas removed his hand, Hannah spoke. "My husband told me often that I worked too hard."

"He was a smart man." Charles Hibbard had found a true jewel in this pile of rocks called Salem. Nicholas could not help but inquire further. "Did you love him, or was it an arranged marriage?"

"That is quite a personal question."

"I am a very nosy man."

A calmness came over Hannah, and she began to knead the bread, but in a softer fashion. "No matter what you've been told, marriages here are not arranged. We are certainly guided, but the choice is ours. I have lived in the village all my life. I knew Charles since I was a girl. We took a liking to each other as we grew and we were very happy for near fifteen years."

"What sort of man was he?"

"Kind. And not nosy."

"Will you remarry?" If she thought him nosy, he may as well be nosy.

"I do not believe I have the heart to do it again."

Nicholas did not doubt the truth in those words. "What happens when a young man and woman of your faith take a liking to one another?"

"If their parents agree, a wedding is arranged." Tilting her head, she caught his eye. "Before the wedding the couple may bundle."

"Bundle? Like, tie their hands?"

When Hannah met his eyes, he saw a smirk on her lips. "A couple is allowed to share a bed before marriage. That is what we mean by bundling."

Nicholas gulped. "Are they asking for trouble?"

"It is a chaste night," Hannah insisted. "A board is placed between the two. The girl's legs may be even be bound together to protect her virtue."

Nicholas could not help laughing. "Oh, but you underestimate young men and women."

Nicholas snapped his fingers and pointed at her, eyes wide. "Did you and your Charles bundle?"

He expected her to brush the question off. "We did. Does that shock you?"

Pretending to laugh even harder, Nicholas moved back toward his seat at the table away from her. It was hard to swallow. All he could think of was Hannah lying in a wooden bed, feeling the stirrings of first desire, and waiting for a man to join her. Chaste night, his ass. "I'd have thought you Puritans smarter than that. Two young people with desire behind them can accomplish a great number of things regardless of bindings. Here I thought you were all cold as fish."

"Perhaps you don't know everything." Hannah wiped her hands on her apron. "Within a marriage, the act of physical love it something to be enjoyed thoroughly." Suddenly the room was warmer than it had been. Was it just him? Nicholas sat back at his papers and let the table hide the growing evidence of his imaginings. "Marriages have been annulled because one or the other person was not satisfying the other in the marriage bed."

Nicholas let a soft groan at the tightness of his trousers.

"What?"

"Nothing."

Hannah knew she'd come out the winner in that discussion. She knelt to set her bread pan into the low embers. "Have you ever thought that it is you who may be wrong?"

"What could I possibly be wrong about?"

"Your complete insistence that none of this is God's will. Perhaps it is your soul, rather than that of the accusers, that needs this reckoning. Perhaps that is why you've come here."

That was utter foolishness, but the words were bold of her to speak. "I came because the Nurse family raised a stink and it won't do for an innocent woman to be hanged." Rising, he began gathering his things. "It should be clear as day to you by now that my blackened soul is charred as those ashes."

Hannah knelt by the hearth. "Even in ashes there can be found a spark."

If only she knew.

If Hannah Hibbard had been a woman anywhere else but Salem Village, he'd have crushed his lips to hers and swam in the sweetness of the kiss once she gave it back. If she allowed and wanted, he'd have taken her there on the floor in front of the fireplace, hard and rough, frustration seeping out until both of them reached sweet release.

This would not be like that. For both their sakes it could not be.

They were from two different worlds.

Holding his papers over the front of his breeches, Nicholas went to his room. "Good night, Mrs. Hibbard."

"Good night, Mr. Cleary."

He left her by the hearth and spent himself into a handkerchief before bed, thinking of women he'd shared his bed with in his past, warm and ample women who had laughed loudly and challenged him in all manner of philosophical and literary discussions. Bernadette and Alice and Ophelia. Yet, he only reached satisfaction when the image of a copper-haired woman in a coif came to mind.

After a while he heard the creak of her bed as she settled in her own quarters.

He felt the filth of his soul when he imagined that the good widow was doing similar while thinking of him. There'd be no saving his soul.

Chapter Five

On the twenty-eighth of June, Sarah Good stood in the Salem Town meetinghouse before the court in a terrible state, even for her. Sarah was never a woman to put care into her appearance, but now months of confinement in jail and the loss of her infant while in said jail bore down on her like a great weight. Her ragged clothes, unwashed appearance, and deep-lined scowl gave her the appearance of one much older than her thirty-eight years.

Seated at a long table before Sarah Good were the judges who would hear her case. Nine successful men given the Governor's permission to wield lives as they saw fit. Judges Samuel Sewall, Jonathan Corwin, Bartholomew Gedney, John Hathorn, John Richards, Nathaniel Saltonstall, Peter Sergeant, and Wait Winthrop were imposing men, merchants and businessmen in fine clothes with gold buttons. Most imposing of all was Chief Justice William Stoughton, who presided over all.

Hannah knew how it would go before it even began.

The prosecutor, Thomas Newton, read a long list of Sarah's torments and curses. Sarah's inability to stop shouting responses did not help her.

Nor did the wide-eyed and believable testimony of seventeen-year-old Elizabeth Hubbard. Elizabeth talked of pinches and pokes from the woman, of Good's urging Elizabeth to sign her name in the Devil's book. "I was on my way to the Proctor's and saw a wolf. It followed me across the fields, and I knew it to be the familiar of a witch. Of that witch, Sarah Good!"

Elizabeth's story chilled to the bone. To top it all off, the girl had a fit.

A statement from Tituba was read. It further tied the wolf to Sarah, and accused her of more crimes, of being the one to force Tituba into evil, forcing her to pinch the children and even to kill Thomas Putnam's child, which she resisted doing.

In a final stroke, a statement by Dorothy Good was relayed, where the four-year-old girl said her mother had three birds and those birds had hurt the children.

This appearance before the court felt more like a formality.

"Where is Dorothy?" Sally whispered from where she sat pressed close to her mother. Hannah did not mind the closeness. The meetinghouse felt like a fireplace full of sparks waiting to flare. Citizens muttered and rocked all around. Some could barely seem to keep from jumping to their feet. The long table full of judges cast near-constant glances of annoyance to the assembled crowd. In this confusion, Sally's closeness was a comfort.

"Still in jail." The poor child was likely shackled all alone, not knowing when and if her mother would return to her. Hannah sent a quick prayer for her and took Sally's hand in hers.

If any woman was a witch, Sarah Good was the one. Person after person attested to it. When Goody Bibber took the stand to declare she was stabbed in the breast by the apparition of Sarah, it sent the room into hushed whispers.

Sarah protested loudly that she'd never done such a thing, and would never do such a thing to anyone.

Goody Bibber raised something high in the air and it caught the light. "See how I've pulled out the blade she used to wound me!"

A collective gasp filled the room.

Hannah turned to the back of the room. Mr. Cleary would be there observing everything. They had both ridden in Anson's wagon to Salem Town that morning. Surely, Sarah Good's trial would change his mind. After everything on display in the courtroom that morning, he would have to agree that witches were real.

In the days since they had spoken frankly, he had distanced himself. In place of a man, he became a whirlwind, leaving after breakfast and often not returning until nightfall. Where he went and whom he was speaking to were mysteries to Hannah, but he asked her fewer questions now.

Still, she would catch his eyes on her from time to time.

In truth, she did not mind.

Unseen, she watched the frown on his face grow deeper as the proceedings went on. Watched him survey the room and take special note of a person here and there. He watched the girls with great interest, and shook his head slightly when Elizabeth Hubbard fell to the ground and wailed. He stood taller than the men around him, broader, and though they were all just standing, he was somehow more alive than most.

Something inside Hannah twitched. Was it desire?

The tall man met her eyes as if he'd heard her calling to him.

Instead of appearing contrite, even with all the evidence presented in the court, he cocked an eyebrow at her. The heat of fury rose in her belly and she looked away.

A few minutes later a young man called out that the broken piece of blade Goody Bibber held was his own and held up the knife it had broken off.

Hannah did not need to look back to know Mr. Cleary was gloating.

"Goody Bibber," Justice Stoughton called once he had regained control of the raucous room. "This is a court of law. Do not tell lies."

"How could she do something like that?" Sally asked. "She lied."

"Hush," Hannah whispered.

Next to the front of the room came Reverend Parris, and Hannah stiffened. It was Parris that Nicholas thought was the root of these evils. It was him Nicholas had come all this way to charge and accuse.

While Parris was not the Reverend Hannah had wanted, or even the one Salem Village had wanted (three failed Reverends before him had not been good enough either) and he was a man of flaws, Hannah knew it could not all be placed on his shoulders. It was too easy an answer unless Parris was the Devil himself, and he was simply too much of an everyday man to be anything powerful. Even if he had swayed Betty and Abigail, the two girls who lived in his house, there were the other girls and grown women making accusations now. Samuel Parris did not hold that much power in the community. Most people didn't even like him.

While he spoke with seeming sincerity of the sufferings of Betty and Abigail, and reminded the court that during Tituba's confession she had "openly charged" Sarah Good and Sarah Osborne, Hannah took in the room.

There was a fury on every face she did not recognize.

It reminded her of something she'd seen in childhood. A pack of wolves had come from the woods. Her father had ordered Hannah and her mother to the house. The sheep had panicked, but stuck mostly together. One lone sheep, older and injured, fell away from the group and soon found itself surrounded by the wolves.

The way the wolves had looked at that sheep was similar to the way the citizens of Salem looked at Sarah Good. She was the weakest, the most obvious target.

Hannah felt her skin rise into goosebumps.

Countless more people recalled their testimonies or offered new ones.

No one spoke for Sarah, the poor woman.

Finally, Sarah herself was allowed to speak.

"Are there any that have seen me as a witch?" The woman asked in a scratchy voice. "Or is it all but the word of these girls and that slave woman?"

Hannah turned to peek back at Mr. Cleary, but he was gone.

Sarah Good's trial, if you could call it that, unnerved Nicholas in a way he had not expected. In a room filled with so much tension and anger, fear still drove the cart. A scared group of people was capable of anything.

Nicholas walked away before the end of the trial, torn between feeling embarrassed for the poor dupes of Salem, anger at them for not seeing what a circus it all was, and a great pity for Sarah

Good who never had a chance against the waves beating at her.

Unless something darker was at work. Unless they were all enchanted.

No. It was religious fervor combined with backwoods ways stirred together in a pot by a corrupt man with a personal vendetta and a family with a desire for land deeds. The Putnams were now on his list of potential rational causes.

There had to be a rational cause. The Devil wasn't real.

He walked to the river and lay in the grass. He closed his eyes to clear his head.

If he stayed longer than needed in Salem Village, he'd likely start seeing demons too.

Scribbling his thoughts on paper helped, and he returned home to the empty house and continued scribbling in the quiet, stripping down to his waistcoat and shirt because the late June afternoons grew ever warmer. If he could only write the right words in the right combination, the lock could be picked and the mystery solved. There had to be an answer. There simply had to be.

A few hours passed before he heard the widow returning home. Stretching from the table, he greeted her. "Good afternoon."

"You did not stay until the end of the trial."

"I did not need to stay. I had seen enough. That was barely a trial."

Instead of replying, she went to the hearth and picked up a knife. Wordlessly, she went back out the door. Nicholas did not know what to do. He followed after her and saw she'd gone stiffly into the garden around the side of the house facing the thick forest.

The woman obviously wanted to be left alone.

But Nicholas was a nosy man and did not leave her alone. "May I speak plain?"

"Can I stop you?"

"Never in my life have I seen such...theatrics. And I have spent much time at the theater!"

"I hardly expect you to understand. You may as well live on the moon, Mr. Cleary."

She went to her knees in the dirt and began pulling peas and gathering them into her apron with quick fingers. Seeing the way her body bent made him ache. Hours spent like that every day would take her straight posture and curve it. He imagined her an old woman with gnarled hands and sun-leathered skin. "Does this way of life not exhaust you?"

Never did she stop working. "My faith is built on the idea of building a better world. We toil for the Lord and for our eventual forever peace."

"But why would God want a man to work himself to the bone?"

"Spoken like one who has never had to." Hannah looked up at him. "If you want me to answer any more of your questions, you had better get down here and pick peas. Otherwise you might find my kindness and patience has come to an end."

"Would you deprive me of your delicious cooking?"

"I would place a squash on your plate and leave you to fend for yourself."

Nicholas did as he was told, if for no other reason than he'd come to practically drool when he saw her working with venison for her stew. He had dined in fancy restaurants where the chef's skill was inferior to Hannah's ability with a piece of deer.

For the first few peas he was clumsy. He dropped two immediately, but soon got the feel for it and increased his speed. Hannah frowned, her mind clearly not on the vegetation.

Likely she did not realize how much of her hair had come loose beneath her coif.

Anywhere but Salem Village, she would have been a sensation. Her fine features and copper hair seemed too lovely for the dirt she knelt in. It was not hard to imagine her in frilled dresses, in colorful fabrics. But he knew she did not desire those things and would not accept them if they were given as gifts. That was the power of blind devout belief: keeping someone on their knees when they should have been dancing among the stars.

"You are staring at me."

"Has a man never admired you before?"

"Not when he should have been working." Hannah scooted a few more feet away from him. "You are thinking words you would like to say." The words were spoken quietly, but they knelt so close together he heard them nonetheless.

Nicholas swallowed. "I am not certain they are words you would care to hear."

"Go on, then. Unburden your mind."

"You are all fools. Blindly following a man simply because he calls himself a Reverend. Men are corruptible; often the most pious are the most corrupted. They feed on power and exploit it, and Parris is in no position to be presiding over a matter such as this. For God's sake, Hannah, the man bankrupted a sugar plantation. A sugar plantation!"

"Anything else?"

"You are smarter than this, Hannah."

By the use of her name, he got her attention. "You do not understand the faith..."

"The faith makes you blind. There are more demons alive walking around in buckled shoes than there are out in the darkness swirling in magic. The Indians wouldn't be attacking if we all hadn't come here and claimed their land. Hale said this land is sick, and he's right. There's blood just beneath every bit of soil. I wish you would all open your eyes..."

She interrupted him. "And I am to take advice from you. You, who believe in nothing."

That stung. "You don't know what I believe."

"I know you mock what I believe."

He had hurt her. "Mocking was not my intention. But I cannot tolerate hypocrisy, even if it's wrapped tightly around a cross."

She sat back on her heels. He expected her to throw peas at him. "If any woman is a witch, 'tis Sarah Good. You heard the evidence. You saw her."

"I saw children screaming and people telling tales about someone they deem disagreeable. I saw a woman who lost her baby in a filthy prison looking exactly the way a grieving mother would. I saw no actual proof. Yet, I have no doubt Sarah Good will be found guilty of witchcraft. And will it be any different tomorrow when Rebecca Nurse goes before Oyer and Terminer?"

"It will. Will you come and see?"

"I will."

"Good," Hannah got to her feet. "Tomorrow you will see an innocent woman cleared of ridiculous charges. There are witches here, Mr. Cleary, but Rebecca is as pure a woman as exists. I have prayed for her every day since her arrest. God will protect her." She seemed so certain. Not a crack showed in her confidence.

Nicholas feared for her heart. "I hope you are right. I do not intend to be your enemy, Hannah."

For a very long moment she stared down at him. "We are having goose for dinner. If you could finish up that row, I might even serve you some."

Hannah returned to the house.

Nicholas stayed in the dirt. He continued picking the green peas.

He slipped one into his mouth and felt immediate guilt as if he had sinned.

Chapter Six

The following day Hannah and Sally set out for the Salem Town meetinghouse at sunrise to get a better seat. Unlike the crowd assembled for Sarah Good, there would be many supportive faces in the crowd for Rebecca Nurse, and Hannah wanted Rebecca to know she was among them.

Men on one side of the aisle, women on the other, Hannah found a space for herself and Sally to fit at the middle end of a pew. Sally tapped her toes from nerves.

"Mrs. Hibbard."

Hannah spun around, greatly surprised to see Mr. Cleary taking a seat at the end of the bench on the other side of the aisle from her. The man had been gone when she'd waked and she had not been certain he would attend this particular day. "Good day, Mr. Cleary."

Maintaining a strict distance between them was best. The last thing Hannah needed was people talking about the strange widow on the outskirts of town and the handsome stranger in her house.

"Let us see what happens, yes?"

"Yes." She sat up straight and turned to face front. If she looked to the Court, she would not be looking at his freshly shaved jaw and noticing how strong it was.

Susannah Martin's trial was up first. Though she was seventy, same as Rebecca Nurse, Susannah was in good health and walked herself into the room accompanied by guards. The very moment Susannah came in, Mercy Lewis fell to the floor and began screaming in a fit. The other girls did the same.

"Do you know this woman?"

Abigail Williams bent over, tearing at her hair. "It is Goody Martin. She hath hurt me often." The voices of the girls rose in cries and screams. Ann Putnam Jr threw a glove at the woman, wailing. They were good little girls dressed in clean dresses, and it was a horrible sight to behold them writhing and terrified.

Shockingly, Susannah Martin laughed.

"What?" Thomas Newton asked. "Do you laugh at it?"

"Well, I may at such folly."

"Is this folly? The hurt of persons."

"I never hurt man, woman, or child."

Mercy raised a hand toward the woman, pointing. "She hath hurt me a great many times and pulls me down."

It went much the same as Sarah Good's trial had. The reading of accusations was followed by the testimonies of more people who had seen and been tormented by Susannah. The Jury was reminded that Susannah had been accused of witchcraft some twenty years earlier, but that had come to nothing. John Alden said she had bewitched and drowned his oxen. Abigail Williams, Goody Bibber, Mary Walcott, and Tituba's husband John all testified. Justice Stoughton asked each of them to approach her, but all four could not bring themselves to.

"What is the reason these cannot come near you?" Thomas Newton asked.

"I cannot tell," Susannah answered. It may be the Devil bears me more malice than any other."

"Do not you see how God evidently discovers you?"

"No, not a bit for that."

"The entire congregation thinks so."

"Let them think what they will."

Though Susannah spoke clearly and in a pious fashion, even quoting the Bible at a few points, it made no difference. Susannah Martin was found guilty and sent to await her execution.

Hannah could believe Susannah or Sarah Good to be witches, after all she had heard all the evidence and watched the proceedings same as anyone, but she would and could not believe the same of Rebecca.

So when the seventy-one-year old woman, who now appeared frailer than ever before, entered the meetinghouse in noisy chains led by Sheriff Corwin, and the wailing and chaos began again, Hannah sat stunned. Never had Rebecca looked unkempt before in all the years she'd known her.

Rumors had spread of invasive examinations happening to the accused women. Rebecca had challenged the women's jury that examined her body for witch's marks.

The first thing requested was a new physical examination. It was denied.

Next, Ann Putnam Jr stepped up to testify of her torments at Rebecca's hands. The girl looked as innocent as a doll. "I saw the apparition of Goody Nurse."

Thomas Newton nodded to Rebecca. "That woman there?"

"Aye. She did immediately afflict me though I did not know her name. I knew where she sat here in the village meetinghouse."

"What does she mean?" Mr. Cleary whispered to Hannah across the aisle.

Hannah whispered back. "Rebecca is a full covenanted member of the church. They sit up front."

Ann's eyes were big with fear. "She hath grievously afflicted me by biting, pinching, and urging me to write in her book." She meant the Devil's book, and it was a powerful charge coming from such a small girl.

Confessed witches Deliverance and Abigail Hobbs were brought into the court to testify. Seeing them, Rebecca said loudly, "What do these persons give in evidence against me now, they used to come among us."

Unlike at the previous trials, the audience in the meetinghouse was truly divided over Rebecca's guilt or innocence. While many believed Rebecca as guilty as any other, her family had raised quite a group to fight for her innocence. Francis Nurse sat right up front, though he went to his feet many times and kept his hands in fists. "That is Rebecca's husband," she pointed for Mr. Cleary.

"Poor man," he answered.

Abigail Williams said that the apparition of Rebecca had choked her. Elizabeth Hubbard and Mary Walcott testified they had been tormented. Nathaniel and Hannah Ingersoll said that Rebecca had killed a man named Benjamin Holton who suffered fits before he died. Mr. Ingersoll joined Reverend Parris and Thomas Putnam Jr in telling how it was Rebecca who had tortured the girls, and how they had spoken of seeing a man all in black with her apparition, as well as many birds.

"How do you answer these charges?" Chief Justice Stoughton asked.

Rebecca could barely hear. The question was repeated. With all the strength in her frail body Rebecca answered. "I have got nobody to look to but God."

Hannah shivered. The woman told the truth.

Still, her freedom would not come without a fight.

Many spoke in Rebecca's favor, testifying to her good and helpful nature, to her religious convictions and reminding everyone that she was a full member of the church.

Throughout, the Nurse family stayed strong. The subject of the petition was raised, and made an impact on several of the judges.

On and on it went, everything against Rebecca one minute and then in her favor the next. Reverend Parris and others testified as to the results of an examination. All of the accused had gone through it, stripped naked and examined by a group of their own sex in search of a witches mark. When they spoke of the exam, and of a place in a private area of Rebecca's body that had been suspect, the old woman clenched her eyes shut and dropped her head. It was humiliating for a private person to have these details spoken to loudly to the entire town.

Finally the jury was sent out of the room to deliberate. The court observers went outside for a breath of fresh air before everyone returned to their seats.

Sally bolted outside the moment she was able. Hannah wished she could have done the same. Instead, she walked sedately as befitted a woman of her age and position. The fresh outside air enveloped her. She felt the cool breeze and longed to be anywhere else, anywhere there weren't so many people and so many things to think about.

"Let us see if you are correct," Mr. Cleary said as she passed on him on her way back inside when the jury had returned. Hannah debated stepping on his foot.

Chief Justice Stoughton conferred with the jury foreman a moment before announcing, "The jury finds you, Rebecca Nurse…"

The room didn't move.

"Innocent."

For a moment, the noise was deafening. Rebecca took a moment to realize what had happened and then put her head back to look to the heavens as the room filled with sounds of both triumph and anger, rejoicing as well as the unimaginable wailings and screams of the afflicted girls and accusers.

Hannah only heard the good. Innocent. The past few months vanished, her troubles and fears eased. The sleepless nights could end. Even as weak her faith was these days, it had held true. The world was still a good place.

By now, there was no aisle dividing the room in half. In the middle of a sea of bodies, Hannah turned to face her boarder. Genuine surprise showed on his face. "You see," she laughed. "It is like I said. God will protect us."

Laughing, she threw her arms around him and embraced him.

Otherwordly light shone from Hannah's face. At the verdict, she had leapt to her feet in the aisle with such joy that she had grasped his arm and did not even notice. She appeared an angel, glowing in the everyday light.

And then she had embraced him.

Nicholas stood stunned by the feeling of her. He'd have loved to have been able to focus on the warmth of her body and the sweet smell of sage that danced from her. He'd have loved to stay in that happy moment for hours and hours and for everything to be well again, but he could not keep from watching the judges.

For the court to render a verdict that seemed just, took everything he'd thought and crumpled it into a ball of useless paper. Nothing he had seen thus far had led him to even contemplate that the trials might be reasonable. After everything, had something divine actually intervened?

"You see," Hannah pulled herself away. A wide smile erased the hardness of her usual expression. "There is goodness in this world, Mr. Cleary."

"It would appear so..."

She turned from him to reach for someone else. Nicholas looked to the Grand Jury. All nine men stood speaking together as a group, a flurry of waving arms and arguments. None appeared relieved at the verdict. None of them were happy. Samuel Sewall looked at Rebecca Nurse with a deep frown.

Nicholas' hackles rose.

Rebecca turned to face the room. She saw the faces supporting her, ignored the others, and smiled a kind smile before she kissed her husband and children and grandchildren that rushed to her. Nicholas was close enough to see the gentle wrinkles around her mouth and eyes as she clasped hands with all those who loved her.

This was no witch. This was a woman who had brought a small army of people to rally behind her in this darkest time. Enough people loved her to sign their names in her defense, potentially risking everything and making themselves targets. Hannah had her hands over her mouth and trembled with wet eyes. Sally bounced and cheered.

There was such happiness, such goodness in that one moment. Nicholas saw it, the community of Salem Village as the City on a Hill it aspired to be.

Stoughton banged his gavel. He continued until the room silenced.

"One moment please." The eyes of the room turned to him. "Has the jury considered all the evidence? Did they hear what the accused said when Deliverance Hobbs entered the room? She said *'They used to come among us.'* Deliverance Hobbs is a witch by her own admission. Is that not a confession? Rebecca Nurse, what do you say to that?"

There was a great hullabaloo among the judges and jury. Stoughton spoke animatedly and shook his hands while the prosecutor and Sheriff both charged to the front of the room. Parris scowled again at the whole lot of them. Faced with this, and after more discussion Nicholas could not overhear, the jury left to deliberate again.

"Mother?"

"I don't understand."

Nicholas turned to Hannah and Sally. He should have been gloating. He had been right and there was no reason or kindness in these proceedings. Seeing their stricken faces and the way they clutched one another, all that remained in him was a similar desperation. He very nearly put his arms around them both. It would have been a kindness to be able to shelter them from the ugliness.

Looking lost, Hannah sought his eyes. "What is happening?"

"It appears they are arguing the verdict."

"How can that be?"

"If ever there was a time to pray, Hannah, it is now."

She did. Sally did as well. Time seemed to stretch forever before the jury settled again. Nicholas pulled out his pen and paper and wrote furiously, a letter to be sent off to the Governor in case things went wrong, telling what had happened and demanding a stay for Rebecca Nurse and her family and all of those many people who loved her and were now being tormented by something very much of this earth.

The jury returned.

Rebecca Nurse was found guilty of witchcraft.

The noise in the meetinghouse was deafening. Everyone was on their feet, shouting and pointing, neighbor battling neighbor with spit words and hateful eyes. Men and women, young and old, everyone combined in rage and triumph seemed enough to be able to bring down the rafters.

Demons were real. Nicholas stood among them.

"Rebecca…" Hannah reached out a hand to the woman, who saw her and began to reach for her. Before they could touch, Rebecca was taken away.

People flooded from the meetinghouse in a great cloud of noise. Sally and Hannah joined them, arms around each other supporting their own steps. While the judges adjourned, looking like tired men, Nicholas broke all customs and walked to the front of the room.

"Who are you, sir?" Judge Hathorne shouted. The man's face was bright red.

The tension among the judges was understandable, but Nicholas did not falter. "I am Nicholas Cleary, come from Governor Phips to see about the trial of Rebecca Nurse. The jury rendered a verdict. Why was it not upheld?"

"They had not considered all the evidence," Stoughton replied.

"But they had." What had happened? What sort of power play had changed the game? Nicholas had missed something and he did not like to miss things. "If you hang an innocent woman, the Governor will not approve."

"The Governor knows all of this already, Mr. Cleary. Take your arguments up with him."

"Perhaps the man is right," Judge Sewall said. "Is it not possible that we...?"

"The jury has decided," Stoughton said. "Good day, Gentlemen."

Dismissed as if they were all no more than kitchen help, the judges brushed past Nicholas and out through the chaos of the meetinghouse as if fleeing a fire. They spoke to no one and met no eyes.

Nicholas followed, but it was not to fight further but to find Hannah.

Nicholas saw Sally's white hair and found Hannah had only made it around the side of the meetinghouse where she stood still as a statue as the assembled crowd trickled away.

Approaching as slowly as if she were a newborn fawn, Nicholas was unsure what he could say. When one's whole heart had been filled with goodness and belief, what could be said when it was all turned around and thrown away in only minutes? Her happiness had been so complete and powerful, the downturn must have been shattering. Her eyes were fixed hard on her worn leather shoes.

A ripping feeling seared across Nicholas' chest. If only he could shield her from the evil of men.

Sally ran to him. "I don't understand, Mr. Cleary."

"There's nothing to understand." The words were weak. He couldn't help Sally understand, nor Hannah's shattered heart, nor Rebecca Nurse's dismal fate. Sooner than later, Rebecca would join Bridget Bishop and the others, and there was nothing apart from an act of God to be done.

Sally let a furious sound close to a scream, and ran off.

Nicholas did not blame her or give chase.

The widow shook her head. "Why has God forsaken Rebecca like this? I am more a sinner than she. Why am I free and she is not?"

What sins had she committed? Best he could tell Hannah was a perfect woman. Perhaps she was speaking from desperation more than reason. The frown she wore reminded him of the crack of an eggshell and how one could never put it back again.

"Oh, Nicholas. What's to be done?"

She had called him by his name.

Nicholas swallowed hard. "Come, let's get you home." He put a hand on her back and slowly moved her away from the meetinghouse and out of Salem Village toward the cottage far from all of it that was coming to feel like a home.

Chapter Seven

The only conclusion Hannah's spinning mind could find was that something evil had settled over all of Salem like a rooftop formed of darkness and evil. Why else would Rebecca's fate be taking her down a road toward the direction of an execution as if she were no better than a cursing beggar woman?

Hannah did not know how she crossed the miles between the courthouse and home apart from the strong arm of Nicholas that led her. She could not recall the way they came or what happened to Sally along the way.

Time seemed to stop. The world stopped.

Hannah felt her heart was ice being carved.

Nicholas brought Hannah into the house, and said something to her she did not hear. She only knew he was there with his hands on her shoulders. His large, strong hands. His handsome face, creased and troubled now. His words, spoken loud, surrounded her like a barricade and she welcomed the safety. Then he went out the door and closed it behind him.

Only once she was alone did she bend over the counter and let go the sob that had lodged in her throat.

Hannah screamed with grief. It felt as if a hundred sewing needles were being thrust into her, as if a thousand wolves were tearing her apart. This must be what hell felt like. Even when Charles had passed she had not felt this terrible. His fever had come and taken him and not lingered and it was simply a thing that happened to people, good or bad. It had made sense, whereas this was senseless.

Screaming helped, but she still felt as if she would burst if she did not do something more than wallow. Clapping her hands together, Hannah went to her hearth. Tied in bundles all around the fireplace were herbs and flowers she had dried. They made sense to her, these vines and leaves and petals. Standing on tiptoe, she pulled down a bundle of basil. The familiar feel and scent of the basil and the gingerroot she grabbed next filled her nose.

When there was dirt beneath her fingernails, the world made more sense.

Sitting would help no one. She would make charm pouches for those closest to her. Sally would get one first, for the girl was a little strange all on her own, and then Anson would need one. Hannah would sleep with one beneath her pillow.

Yes, that was it. She would make them safe.

There had been a full moon the night before and she had set water out in bowls to absorb the energy the moon provided. Quickly, she washed her hands in the water, sprinkled a few drops over her counter, and got to work.

First she mixed chamomile for peace, dill for preservation, and mint for wisdom. Then she swirled in a large amount of sage and clover for protection, and a handful of salt to ward off evil. Hannah sharpened her knife and chopped the plants, mixed them, and packed them tight into small folded pieces of fabric. Into each she also placed an acorn for luck. Needle in hand, she began to sew shut the pouches so they would not spill. She barely looked up from her herbs and needle and thread when Sally returned a while later, red-faced from either crying or running. Mother and daughter looked at each other and there was nothing to be said. The girl took it upon herself to make plates of bread, cheese, and pickles and to put one next to Hannah and one at the seat Nicholas had taken to sitting at. He had not yet returned. Sally wordlessly took her own plate upstairs.

The day had faded to night before Nicholas returned, missing his jacket and with his collar open.

"Hannah," he said as he rubbed at his eyes.

She nodded at him. His eyes were darker now. The original judgment she had set upon him was entirely wrong. He was not distant or untouched by the events. The arrogance she had seen on his arrival was gone. Now he was unraveled same as she was, and it would take a stronger woman than Hannah was to ignore his fearsome beauty.

"You look as if you've done battle."

"The wind picked up. I thought I…" But whatever he'd thought, he didn't finish his words. He shook his head, then shook it again, and kept shaking it as he moved to his seat at the table. For a long moment, he stared at the plate Sally had made him.

Hannah picked up another piece of fabric to make a new charm. This one would be for him. The poor man needed one as badly as she did.

More thread on her needle, more dried green on the wood of the counter. Stitch by stitch, hole by hole, she would sew them all to safety.

"You will go blind stitching in the dim light. Come over here. Come share my candle." Nicholas gestured her to the table, where he had finished his plate of food and again covered his space with papers and ink.

Hannah had stood sewing for hours in the same place. Now her neck was stiff and her feet ached. She gathered her things and went to the seat next to him. They were very close, but the light shone brightest in that spot. "Thank you."

"Someone may as well get use from it. It is a waste of time for it to light my hand tonight." He tossed the pen onto the table and set his head back against the tall chair. "I did not think I could be surprised anymore. But today's verdict…"

"Where did you go?"

"I walked."

"Where?"

Nicholas thought for a moment. "I do not recall. I walked as if I could walk into the answer and the truth, but it was all for naught."

"What will you tell the Governor?"

"That it is all wrong. What would you have me tell him?"

Hannah ceased sewing and considered her words. She wanted to tell him to run to Boston and scream to the Governor for a rescue. But if this was truly God's will, then what would be the point? Could salvation come in the form of a man who was not of this faith and who worked for the very government that had brought the court to the precipice of good or evil it wobbled on? It was the Governor who had established the Court.

Hannah doubted Governor Phips' ability to lead through these times.

Again, she doubted God. In that doubt, she felt the Devil.

Hannah put her needle back to the cloth. "I do not know what you should tell him, for I do not know what is happening."

"What is that you are making?" He had bent his head close to her own. If she had been bolder, she would have tucked her head onto his strong shoulder and rested there, let the troubles of the world pass by, safe in her walls and his strength.

"It is my hope that they will bring luck."

"That you can still hope is a miracle, Hannah. You are a miracle."

When she brought her eyes to his, she expected to see something like seduction following his words, but there was only sincerity there. He admired her as a person and a woman, and Hannah felt her heart swell. "I do not much like to wallow. And I would like to believe that miracles are still possible."

Nicholas slowly moved his hand to hers and patted it. "I as well, Hannah."

Nicholas was not a man unaccustomed to strange things and yet this town was unlike anything he'd known. People gone wild, women swinging from trees, the Devil walking among them, and yet an undercurrent of something more, but what? Underhanded greed? Repressed lust? Carnality? Men in the new world were rumored to take to relations with beasts. It shouldn't have shocked him, but at his center he felt as if he'd never been a part of the world before. He tried rational explanations and wild ones, each one a new spray of ink on paper, and for each one that became a letter bound for the Governor, there were five that wound up crumpled on the wood planks of the floor before he handed them to Hannah to put in the fire.

In the days that followed Rebecca Nurse's verdict, he wrote.

No matter how many words he put to paper, nothing changed.

He returned to the courthouse and listened to other trials. Two more women, Sarah Wilds and

Elizabeth Howe, were tried and found guilty. More accusations came. A slave woman called Candy and her mistress, Margaret Hawkes, were both accused by Thomas Putnam. There was word Candy had pointed the finger at her own mistress and detailed how she had used poppets to curse others.

The madness continued to spread.

The demons in the rafters never quieted.

Hannah quieted. Dark circles formed beneath her eyes as she moved through her daily tasks, always with a creased brow but never leaving anything to wait. She made candles and tended the garden and canned things and cooked delicious food, but he had been close enough to her in the past weeks to see how she held a twister inside her.

If she could only have raged. It would have relieved her. But the confines of her society would not allow that.

Days passed in a sick, solemn quiet. Nicholas fell asleep most nights thanks to his supply of rum.

One night, Hannah did not come in from the garden. Nicholas put the kettle over the fire to heat water for tea and realized how dark it had become, so he went to see if she was well.

He found her seated in the garden, watching the moon.

It seemed as good a thing as any to do, so he joined her.

"I did not realize it had gotten so late." She stirred as if she had been enchanted.

"Do not rush inside on my account."

She stilled. Nicholas pulled up his knees. "May I ask you something that I have long wondered?" Hannah nodded her head. "Pardon me for saying it, but you seem different from the others here."

"I suppose you mean me for me to think that a compliment."

"I most certainly do! By God, Hannah, you're sensible. You're even rational most of the time. I sit in that meetinghouse and that courthouse and I listen to people being entirely foolish and I cannot help wonder how you are as you are in the middle of all this." She actually chuckled at that, and he felt lightness at being able to lighten her load of sorrow.

"That is just how things are."

"I don't entirely believe that is how you are."

She sighed deeply. The lovely face was easier here, the frown gone. She was an astonishing beauty when she wasn't frowning. Though if he was admitting it, he even enjoyed her frowns, for these were certainly times to frown about.

"My mother and my grandmother taught me about plants from the time I was a girl," she began. "They came here from England before I was born, for they were gossiped about."

"Was your mother a witch?"

"She did many things that a witch is said to do. I don't believe she signed a Book of the Devil in her own blood, but she knew the plants and the stars and the old medicines. If that's magic, then she was a witch, as I must be. But in this new world, she held that back. She put on these clothes and disappeared into this world, and my father loved her though he was fooled by how good she was at pretending."

Nicholas could not take his eyes from her. "And you and Charles were the same?"

"Aye. He knew about the plants, though. But I never shirked my duties, and he found it an amusing hobby."

So there were even secrets in this house in Salem. "I'd noticed the herbs. I also noticed the line of salt around the house and the pouch you placed beneath my mattress."

"You are to keep it there and one on your person until I tell you otherwise. They are made of mint and sage and other things for luck and peace. I need something to do with my hands or my mind wanders to terrible places as it has this night." Dusting off her hands, she got to her feet.

Genuinely surprised and touched, he teased. "Thank you. I figured I'd be the first to go."

Hannah stood over him. "You are a good man. Well, if not a *good* man, then you at least mean well."

"Do I? I came here certain I'd nail Parris to the cross, solve all of this and go home glorious. Now, there's no glory. There's no one crime to solve." He rose as well.

"Were you so certain you could fix all this? Nicholas, you are one man."

"Call it arrogance, but yes."

"I am sorry for that."

"Do not feel sorry for me. I, at least, will not go to the gallows. I will, in this moment, stand here under this moon with a woman I find fascinating."

A wisp of hair blew across Hannah's cheek.

As if screaming the frustration Nicholas could not express, the kettle began to whistle. Both rushed into the house to pull it from the heat before the noise woke Sally. Hannah poured the hot water into two mugs she quickly readied with loose leaves. "Let them sit a few minutes to steep."

They stood together by the fire's warmth. The room was warm enough already in the late summer heat with the windows open. The flickering flames danced against Hannah's face.

Before he could retrieve the senses that left him, Nicholas set his hand on hers.

It was an audacious move. He anticipated a hard slap.

Instead, their two hands rested together. There was a little peace.

"Mr. Cleary…"

"There is no need to call me by a formal name anymore."

Hannah moved her hands to her mug and held it in front of her. The frown had returned. "Nicholas. We mustn't become too familiar."

"I understand and I apologize."

"It's not that I don't…"

He was too eager. "Want to?"

"No. Yes. Oh, you." She swatted him like she would a fly and put her hands around the stone mug. "What I may or may not want doesn't matter right now. I have to think of Sally. All too easily she could wind up without a mother, and then who would she have in this world? These are not times to entertain flirtations with handsome men."

His heart gave a gigantic thump and he nearly knocked over his tea. Perhaps while he had been admiring her, she had been similarly admiring of him.

Nicholas picked up his tea and blew on it as he went back to his seat. "I will comfort myself knowing you think me handsome and did not attempt to knock my head off for my forward gesture. Also, you have my word that I will keep your secret. As far as I can say, you are simply a God-fearing widow who likes plants too much."

Hannah smiled gratefully. "Thank you. I appreciate that more than I can say."

"You are most welcome."

A moment passed. "Besides, you'll be leaving soon," she said quietly.

Was that sadness in her voice? "Will I?"

"After all, isn't Rebecca why you came to Salem? Any day now I expect her death warrant to be signed."

Nicholas had longed to leave Salem Village from the moment he'd arrived. While he watched Hannah and the way she stared too hard at her tea, he realized that the things he had wanted to get back to, his room and his things and his foolish construct of a life were not real and true things. Boston would not miss him. But he would miss Hannah. He would miss the way his seat at the table and the smell of the herbs that had seeped into the walls of the house had come to feel comfortable.

"I'd like to believe her story isn't over yet."

It was not a big smile he brought to her face, but it might as well have been the sun. Even in all the darkness, Hannah still had hope.

Nicholas turned away and went to his room before he wept at his lack of it.

Chapter Eight

The long way into the village took Hannah past the pond, and she slowed her pace. Unable to stop the smile that came to her mouth, she picked up a flat stone and skipped it across the water like she had as a girl.

Hope was a funny thing. After hoping with all her soul for goodness, one tiny bit of sunshine had broken through the clouds.

Governor Phips had granted Rebecca Nurse a reprieve.

The world did not stop moving and the trials continued, but at least there was one little piece of light in all the misery. Not three days after the tragedy of Rebecca being excommunicated from the Salem Town church, the Nurse family had shouted in joy as the piece of paper granting her a stay of execution had arrived. She would stay in jail, but at least she was not being rushed toward the gallows anymore.

Hannah felt like a feather floating in the breeze. She felt like dancing.

She had left Sally at home with pen and paper and the Bible. Nicholas had started helping Sally improve her reading and letters and the two of them had formed a friendship. They were two clever people. Hannah could not read much more than her Bible and could write only a little, but Sally had a bright mind and could be something more.

The crisp air and the ripples of flowing water calmed her. Fisherman went across the pond and Hannah watched them. She had never been on a boat. What if she sailed away on a ship with Sally and never returned to Salem? She could find work sewing or tending house for someone. Perhaps Sally could go to school.

What was it like in Boston where Nicholas lived? Things were fancier there, of course, but were things better?

Despite Rebecca's reprieve, the man was still at her home with no plans to leave. He remained deeply suspicious of Parris and concerned for Dorothy Good. In recent days, he had become obsessed with the trial of Candy, the slave woman with the poppets. His heart was drawn to the disadvantaged.

It was all too clear now that had been wrong about him.

The July breeze swept around her as she gathered dandelions.

Casting a quick glance around and seeing no one, Hannah took the time to pray for Sally and Anson and all the people who had been her neighbors these years, for Rebecca and Sarah and Dorothy Good and the Proctors and all those in jail. She prayed for the girls to find an end to their troubles, whatever that meant. She prayed that the judges would be enlightened and see the truth.

Then, she prayed for herself.

God forgive me, but I question my place in Salem. Is it your will I should stay here among this trouble and uncertainty? I have never felt I belonged here, but is this your plan for me? Or should I leave and seek a better and Godlier life in a place without all these scars upon it?

She waited for an answer. One did not come.

Hannah turned from the pond and walked on. Just outside the village she heard someone call her name.

The voice was not at all divine. It made her want to retch.

Harmon Webb strode toward her in a fine suit of dark gray, wearing a grin.

It was funny how Nicholas Cleary, who was not at all a Puritan, was a good man while Harmon

Webb, who was a pillar of their community, was a bother.

"Ah, I thought that was you there."

"Aye, 'tis me. Good morning." She started to walk toward the center of the village, hoping she could lose him, but he fell into step with her.

"I have heard about Rebecca."

He was going to say more, so Hannah's reply was wary. "Indeed."

"It is an interesting development. The reprieve, I mean. Still, those who make deals with the Devil should know they have it coming." Harmon's walking stick hit the earth with emphasis. Hannah clutched her basket tighter and resisted arguing. "I think it's good, these trials. Rooting out the evil among us and sending them where they belong."

"Where people belong is not for us to decide. Rebecca is as pious a woman as there is."

He raised an eyebrow as if surprised to hear her raise an objection to something he had said. Most Puritan women of her poor station would not have raised an objection to a man of his wealth. "But she was found guilty, was she not?"

"Yes. She was."

"Then there it is. The Lord would not have found her so if she was not a witch."

"Perhaps the Lord had nothing to do with it."

Harmon's eyes grew wide. He stepped a bit closer. "Do you not think it's a miracle that they've all been rooted out so easily? One word from a small girl and," he snapped his fingers. "It is done."

"At least Rebecca has been saved."

"Are you so certain? I hear it is still being discussed. Justice Stoughton did not appreciate the trouble at her trial. I would wager that she'll be dead before the month is out."

The vile man was so certain that the words coming from his mouth were true. A bitter taste came into Hannah's mouth. Though she knew she should hold her tongue, she could not. "How dare you speak of her that way?"

Hannah grabbed her skirt and turned to storm away.

"Best make sure that no one mentions you, Hannah, as someone worth looking into."

Like many times before, Hannah wished herself a witch—a real witch, a fearsome one—so she could choke him without notice. The past weeks had made her bolder, and less accepting of nonsense. "Do you so lust for my land that you would condemn me to death for it?"

Her blunt words had infuriated him. Harmon lunged forward, grabbed her elbow and held it too hard. She knew his fingers would bruise. "I would sooner have you as my wife, to have both your land and you, but I will do what I can. Examine your position: a widow, alone, and Charles' death was so sudden."

Those words lingered. A chill traveled all along Hannah's body. "It was a fever."

"Perhaps. Perhaps it was you, under an evil hand. Is Hannah Hibbard a name written in the Book of the Devil? Perhaps I should ask Betty Parris."

"Betty is a confused child."

One eyebrow rose. "She is easily persuaded. Just like little Ann Putnam and the rest. You grow too brave, Hannah."

"Mr. Webb!" A voice interrupted them and Hannah pulled her hand back to her basket. The call had come from Reverend Hale. Thank goodness, Nicholas was walking with him. The two men walked together every day, Nicholas had said.

Harmon smiled as if nothing untoward had occurred. "Ah, Reverend. How are you this day?"

Hale held out his hands. "Well. Mrs. Hibbard, good morning to you."

The Reverend from Beverly smiled at her, and Hannah knew she was safe. The two men came closer and Hannah saw how Nicholas looked at Harmon. Displeasure showed clearly on his face and he knew already something was wrong.

"Mr. Cleary and I were discussing Rebecca Nurse."

"That seems to be all anyone can talk about today," Harmon practically spit.

"What else should they be talking of, sir?" Nicholas stood equally tall to Harmon. "Of what interest are suppers or town gossip in the face of a woman's life being spared?"

Harmon scoffed and made as if to walk past them. "The writer from Boston, I assume."

"I am."

"Might I suggest you keep your opinions on matters that don't concern you to yourself?"

Nicholas shrugged his shoulders. "Of course. But these matters concern me very much. The Governor sent me here to sniff out the evils taking place." He said it such that there could be no doubt the trials were not entirely the matter he meant.

"And what evils are those, Mr. Cleary?"

"There are a great many things that stink around here, Mr. Webb. I will see Mrs. Hibbard home." Nicholas stared at Harmon. When he at last turned to face Hannah, he gave a small wink and suggested a path in the opposite direction Hannah had come with a hand. Hannah bid Hale farewell quickly. The Reverend made no effort to walk with Harmon, going southwest even though Hannah knew that direction could not possibly take him anywhere he would want to go. Not that she could blame Reverend Hale.

Once they were out of earshot, Nicholas sneered, "Who was that?"

"That is Harmon Webb. He is a wealthy local merchant with a very high opinion of himself."

"Does he want to court you?"

"He would like to marry me without any courtship, thereby taking possession of my land."

"I think he would like more than that."

Hannah blushed a little. "He is fooling himself if he thinks I will consider him, Mr. Cleary. I would sooner drink the sludge from the shore of the creek."

Mr. Cleary bent his head toward her. "Please call me Nicholas. Are you truly alright?"

"Yes, thank you."

"Would you like me to hit him?"

Hannah's stifled a laugh. "That won't be necessary."

"Are you certain? It would be a pleasure. Too bad you're not a witch."

"I think that almost every day." Hannah gasped.

The words were too familiar. The ease she felt when she was with him was risking too much. She needed to think of Sally and cease wading into dangerous waters. What good was a mother swinging from the gallows to her daughter?

They walked in a big circle from the village back around Cedar Pond. Nicholas bent for a rock and picked it up, then threw it as far over the water as he could. She could call him Nicholas. They were at least that familiar. Hannah picked up a flat rock and skipped it expertly.

Nicholas started. "Was there something you needed back in town? I could fetch it for you if you'd like to avoid Mr. Webb."

"Nothing I cannot get tomorrow." For all she wanted was to stay where they were, safe in that quiet moment with the ripples on the water. Hannah gazed for one moment upon him, knowing in another world there could have been something between them greater than the gray world. Nicholas moved until he stood by her side.

Their arms touched. How she wanted him.

Hannah knew in that moment that he needed to leave Salem Village. No matter how good he was and how much she enjoyed him beside her, he was no part of her world and did not want to be. For his sake she had to help him reach his conclusions so he could leave and she could go back to before. "If you would like to speak to Sally, you may."

He stumbled, he moved so quickly turning to her. "Hannah!"

"I trust you. I know your intentions are good. I cannot offer anything to help you, but maybe she can. Sally ventures into the village far more than I do."

"Thank you," he gushed. "That might be just the thing. Sally is likely to know the sort of things that would be kept away from the eyes of adults. If I can ascertain the root of the girls' behavior, maybe I can follow the vines of it…"

Hannah ignored the excited sparkle in his eyes.

Impulsively, Nicholas took her shoulders in his hands and kissed her forehead.

It was like heaven. And it was terrible.

It had been too forward, the kiss.

Hannah had not spoken the rest of the way home. Nicholas wanted to say something, but the moment Hannah had allowed him to question Sally, his mind had jumped into a whirlpool of questions he should ask. Sally offered a unique perspective. The girls who had started this were her contemporaries. He had watched Abigail Williams, Betty Parris, Mercy Lewis, Mary Walcott, and the others since he'd arrived, and had no good answers for why they behaved as they did. Sally was a good girl, smart as a whip and honest to a fault. It could be just the step Nicholas needed to discover something that could help.

That very evening, Hannah made dandelion tea and called Sally to the table.

The girl came as called, fiddling her fingers as if she thought she was in trouble. An expression of fear rested on her face, but Hannah quickly set a hand on her daughter's shoulder. "You are in no trouble. You know that Mr. Cleary is here to write about the accusations and the hangings."

"Yes," Sally whispered.

"He would like to ask you a few questions. That is all."

"What have I to say about it?"

Hannah gestured to Nicholas. She allowed him to begin. "Sometimes a new pair of eyes is needed to look at a problem. Your mother and I and many others have tried to solve this one, but clearly we have failed. Perhaps you hold the key to a solution without even knowing it."

"I'm just a girl."

"Never discount yourself so. Joan of Arc was just a girl."

"Who is Joan of Arc?"

Of course she was ignorant of the history. "She was a French girl not much older than you. She had a vision from God and led the French army to victory at Orleans. Never discount the power of girls. After all, all of Salem has been brought to their knees by them."

Sally looked at him with excited eyes. "What happened to Joan of Arc?"

Nicholas immediately regretted his example. "She was burned at the stake."

Sally looked to Hannah. "Mother?"

Hannah shot Nicholas a look. "You are safe. No one is burning anyone at any stakes around here. Answer what Mr. Cleary, Nicholas, asks. I will be right here." Then she stepped back to her table and her herbs. Nicholas was grateful for the trust she put in him, though he knew she would listen to every word.

He picked up his pen. "Are you friends with the afflicted girls? Abigail Williams, for starters? She seems among the loudest."

Sally wrinkled her nose. "As much as anyone can be."

"What do you mean by that?"

She gave a little shrug. "Abigail is not easy to befriend. Betty either."

That was interesting. The girls had been portrayed as perfect darlings by the adults he'd spoken to, innocent little angels put upon by terrible demons. "Tell me more."

"They think themselves better than I. "

"Because you're poor?"

"Yes." Sally did not even blink at his blunt question.

"Let me tell you a secret, Sally. Rich people are often far more miserable than the rest of us. All the gold in the world cannot ease a troubled soul. Now, you are the same age as the girls and, for lack of a better word, you are friends with them, yet you are not afflicted."

"I am not."

"Why do you think that is?"

Sally picked at a small fray by her knee on her dress. "I do not doubt in God, and there is nothing I desire so much as to make me turn from that." The bright light of certainty shone from her, a good and pretty Puritan girl who would never face the struggles of those considered outsiders. Even if she didn't know it, that was a sort of privilege worth more than gold.

"You have never danced in the woods?"

Hannah looked up. "Nicholas!"

"It is a common rumor. The girls dance in the woods."

Sally shook her head. "Mama has told me to keep from the woods, so I do."

Hannah nodded. "There are many dangers out there. Real ones."

"Elizabeth Hubbard was followed home by a wolf," Sally reminded him.

"So I've heard her tell," Nicholas said. Sally had all her mother's hard-set determination and he imagined it would take a great deal for her to succumb to nonsense and riddles. "Tell me, and I hope the answer comes from the mouth of a babe, how do you account for the other girls? Why is it that when one screams, they all scream and flail and seem to answer as one voice, if not for the Devil's influence?"

"I did not say it was not the Devil's influence," Sally replied.

"But Dorothy Good is only four, and is said to have bitten little Ann Putnam like an animal." Sally giggled before covering her face quickly. "Do you have an answer?"

"Only that a good many of us would bite Ann and Goody Putnam if we had the chance."

Hannah dropped her head, and Nicholas could see that even she was trying not to smile. Sally sat up quickly. "Forgive me, Mr. Cleary. I do not mean to make light."

"If one cannot make light at a time like this, what good is waking up in the morning?"

"Yes, but Dorothy is a sweet child and should not be in jail. I pray for her every night."

"Of course not," Nicholas assured her. "Why do you think Dorothy confessed?"

"She is four."

"Yes."

"If I was four, I'd be scared. I am twelve, and I am scared. If Mother went to jail, I cannot say I would not do the same to be with her." Nicholas went to scribble some observations, but Sally seemed to have more to say. "Grown people often think of children as fools. But there's lots we know, even if they try and hide it from us. Especially us girls. We're around, even if they pretend we aren't. Dorothy is a bright child and lots of people don't like her mother. It's funny how some people simply don't fit and even people who think themselves kind don't like them for it." Nicholas understood better than most how even people who declared themselves good could still find ways to think of other people as lesser, and thereby treat them abominably. "Have I said something wrong?"

"On the contrary, my dear."

"Might I be excused, Mother?"

"Of course."

"Good night, Mother," Sally kissed her mother's cheek before going up to bed. "Good night, Mr. Cleary."

"Good night, Sally." As Sally went up her ladder out of sight, Nicholas pointed after her. "She would be a fine lawyer, you know."

"She will likely marry in the next few years and make a home for her husband and children." Hannah passed the table and handed him a piece of rye bread with creamy butter spread over the top.

"And that will be enough?"

"It is the way it is. Did you learn anything from her?"

All the things Sally said rolled around in Nicholas' mind, forming new thoughts. "Fear is a powerful force. Combine the fear of the French and the Indians with the fear of the Devil and with these girls who believe God will smite them should they do a wrong, and the few of them who have survived terrible tragedies, and it's a recipe for a sick stew that might just turn into something like…."

He took a big bite of the bread and chewed it, savoring the rich flavors.

It could all make for something very ugly. It *had* all made for that.

"Still, I will say this," he continued. "I am glad that of all the homes in this ridiculous rock pile of a village fate put me in yours. I doubt anyone else would make such wonderful bread."

"Anyone else would have thrown you out."

"Likely." Acknowledging her tease, he smiled. "But also here I do not feel as if I must keep myself secret. I can speak freely with you."

"And what sort of things would you say?"

"Were the world different, Hannah, I daresay you might be a rebel." She stopped by his seat, and he stood up.

147

The way she brought her gaze over him did not escape him. "I am going to bed. And tonight I will pray for a good long while."

"Over me?"

"You flatter yourself, Mr. Cleary." She used his formal name in jest, and he saw the way her eyes seemed to sparkle in the candlelight.

"Am I not worthy of your prayers?"

"There are not enough hours in the day for all the prayers you would need."

"I believe you think me far worse than I am," he said in a soft whisper, and took her fingers in his own. Hers were rough from her daily work, but it was marvelous.

"'Tis not my judgement you should concern yourself with."

"Do you ever desire more than this?"

Whatever she desired, he would give. She had simply to say the words.

To his great surprise, and delight, Hannah raised her hand to touch his cheek. He still held her other hand, and brought her fingers up so he could lightly brush a kiss against her knuckles.

The sweet moment was interrupted by a pounding on the door.

A knock on the door at that late hour could not be good. After jumping like a rabbit, Hannah ran to the door to admit Anson. The old neighbor moved quickly, his coat spackled with the light rain that had begun falling.

"Bittner," Nicholas crossed the room. "What is it?"

"Nothing good," Anson replied. "Come to tell you the death warrant has been signed for Rebecca. She'll hang on the twelfth, with Good, Martin, Howe, and Wilds."

Hannah put a hand to her mouth. "But she was reprieved!"

Anson nodded. "And now it's been reversed."

Nicholas felt fire light in his belly. "Who reversed it?"

"Governor Phips."

Nicholas had written the Governor over and over regarding the matter. Now he and everyone else had been fooled by the fragility of men. He saw the disappointment on Hannah's face and felt it as though he had caused it.

"Anson…" Hannah managed. "Say it isn't true."

"I wish I didn't speak true."

Hannah and Anson embraced. Unable to hold in his fury, unable to understand this tragic turn, Nicholas shouted to the room. "But there is

149

no proof. All they have it stories and specters. There is no tangible proof!"

Anson spoke over Hannah's shoulder. "This is Salem Village, Mr. Cleary. We don't need proof anymore."

Chapter Nine

Before she erupted in a scream that tore down the house and blew away the village, Hannah grabbed candles and matches and went out the back door of the house into the rainy night the moment Anson left.

Here and there, the crescent moon peeked through clouds. Hannah wished she had the ability to run all the way to that moon. Instead, she ran until her lungs ached and her hair stuck wet from the rain to her forehead. Along the way her coif slipped. She left it behind. Wet strings of hair loosened from her long braid fell in her face as her feet pounded the wet grass, but Hannah did not stop running until was safe in the forest.

Once hidden by the branches, she went immediately to the spot where the fire had burned. That terrible spot.

She had come there for a reason. Dropping to her knees by the remnants of ash, she set up a circle of candles and tried to light matches. She would try a ritual with candles she had seen her mother do once on a hot August night when the town had been besieged by illness, though Hannah had never tried something like this and knew she'd be clumsy and unpracticed. Maybe it would do good. It could hardly do any more harm.

The matches would not light.

She threw one down. Tried another. Another.

With a roar of frustration, she hurled them away and fell to her knees. A great sob erupted from her soul, up though her throat and into the world. It was a primal sort of scream, and the birds ahead flew from branches. Her fingers clawed into the dirt and rocks. Salem had terrible soil. It was a terrible place to make a settlement. By choosing it the first people in the new world had consigned them all to terrible struggle.

Everything was terrible and Hannah was not even enough of a witch to help.

"Hannah."

Nicholas must have run after her when she'd left the house. She'd forgotten him and everything else in her fury and fear, but he had come all this way. It was strange to see him in the woods where she never saw another soul. Soaked, he stood before her. The cotton of his shirt stuck to his shoulders.

Why was he the man that he was? Why could he not have been horrible? "You should not have followed me."

"On the contrary, I think I had every right to. Here now," Nicholas approached and reached for her, seeming stunned by her ferocious appearance, but she felt no shame. There was no time to be ashamed.

With him a few feet away, she touched the earth. "This is where they danced, you know. Those girls. That's where the fire was lit." Kneeling in the dirt, Hannah indicated the space before her. "It all started with that fire. That spark seared through us all and has scalded all of us. Some were killed and some will live forever with the scars and wounds."

"This is where they are said to have offered themselves to the Devil?"

Hannah sat back and pulled her knees to her chest. "The very spot. My father always used to tell me not to come to the woods, but my mother always came anyway. I am like her."

Nicholas examined the darkened flat place on the ground. "Has the Devil ever appeared to you, Hannah?"

Hannah wiped water from her face. "I am a woman of sound mind. If the Devil had appeared,

I would run the other way. I have too much to do to deal with the likes of him." Not rising from her knees, she scooted to a cluster of stems and pulled her knife to cut them.

"I didn't mean to startle you. I worried when you ran off, so I followed. After all, these are dangerous woods." He saw the fast work of her hands and knife. "What is that you're gathering? Hannah, you have my vow of secrecy."

Her answer was mean, borne of frustration. "This one is for potency. Would you like some?"

"What makes you think I need it?"

Facing away from him, she dropped her hands to her lap. She could barely breathe. The whole of the world and Nicholas besides were too much for any simple woman to take. Rain pushed down on her, and she wished it could just push her into the earth. "You may be tired from the scores of women in your wake."

"I would not say scores of women."

"No need to lie. I envy your freedom." It was a confession she had not expected to make. Rising to her feet, Hannah stuffed the plants in her pockets and wiped her dirty hands on her apron. "Even for us to be alone like this is dangerous."

"But we have done nothing."

"What it true does not matter. Only what people believe matters."

"Would you leave Salem if the opportunity fell into your hands?" Nicholas had somehow, through his own unexplainable magic, come so close she could see the stubble on his jaw even in the darkness. He touched her hand with his own, which held her fingers lightly as he had when he had kissed her fingers not an hour earlier.

Leaving would be the simplest thing in the world. "I had not thought of it."

He ran his thumb over her palm. "Why, Widow Hibbard. I believe that is the first time you have lied to me. Never lie to me."

One did not always make sensible choices when one's heart was troubled. One often fell into foolishness to distract from the true problems of the world.

When Hannah rose on her toes to join her lips to his, it was because the man standing before her, handsome and intelligent and so marvelously warm and with his hard body pressed against hers as he returned the kiss, was a glorious kind of distraction. The kiss was close to heaven. Was it magic?

The most alone they had ever been, at last they found each other.

"What if I were from anyplace else than here?" Hannah managed as he dragged his lips over her neck to the place just below her ear. The hot breath there made her tremble.

"I would not have waited this long to touch you this way, I assure you." Nicholas slid his hands around to lock her against him. Shivers like she had only ever imagined raced over her body. "I didn't know if lightning would strike me for my impertinence."

She pushed back enough to see him. "I am furious with this town. I feel ridiculous. I feel deceived. I feel so many things and each of them gives me thoughts, terrible thoughts."

"I stand on shaky ground as well, Hannah. I am unsettled. I would take a knife to Governor Phips for his deceit in signing the death warrant. I swear I did not think it would go this way."

"I believe you."

Nicholas held her face in both his hands. "Everything is horrible, but when I look at you it is the best kind of madness."

Closing her eyes, she fell against him. What was magic, after all, if it did not include passion? If Hannah's soul was bound to burn for her doubts, she may as well enjoy a few moments with a man who wanted to spend the same moments with her. No one would be hurt.

Nicholas dropped to his knees, clutching at her wet skirts.

She met him down in the dirt and ash.

More kisses came, yearning kisses, explosive ones that shook the foundations of the life Hannah knew. This wasn't the path she had started out to take, but it was the direction she now chose for herself.

Though he could barely see Hannah in the hard rain, he followed her.

He followed as her coif came off and her hair fell down. The braid went past her waist and a wink of moonlight showed him its lush color. For too long he had wanted to know the feel of her lips. God and the Devil and the Governor be damned, he needed to know her and how she felt and tasted.

Lightning did not strike him. He did not burst into flames.

With his lips against her shoulder as they knelt together in the wet dirt, he felt her breath in his ear. "You should never have come to Salem Village."

Nicholas agreed. "I absolutely should not have."

"I was safe until you." His hands were unloosing her waistcoat stays now. Hannah watched his fingers and did not say a word.

"No one will hurt you," he assured.

"I could be accused."

"Don't think of it," he kissed her again and kept on as if it was possible to kiss away all her fears. "Don't think of anything but here and now. Me. We are here and I know that I could not be happier. Do you feel the same, Hannah?"

In response, Hannah set his hand upon her breast.

"What is it you want?" he asked. "Truly, Hannah tell me what you want and I will give it."

"I want more than this," she glanced to the trees, and he understood. She wanted more than a life in a town like Salem. "I want to be someplace where I do not have to hide myself away and keep quiet. I want to know more than the Reverend will tell me." Nicholas felt the soft weight of the breast and the chill of her rain-dripped skin, the goosebumps that formed as he ran his thumb over the hard bud. Hannah gripped his shoulder harder. "I want…"

"Tell me. I shall give it."

"The girls spin lies," she whispered.

"You believe them to bear false witness?"

"Aye, and it is not only me. I have seen them, and they are certainly sincere in their fear and performance, but…" She took hold of both his shoulders and her eyes pierced through him. "When I was a child, I coveted a beautiful blue stone a friend of mine had. I only wanted to hold it for a moment. One day, I took it from her, and I was caught. Fearful of punishment, I found myself spinning lies I did not even think before I spoke—that the stone had fallen onto the floor and I was merely picking it up."

"They lied to stop themselves from being punished, and everything since has been false?"

Hannah did not confirm this. "But it is more than that. It is as if now, that they've come this far, they believe their own lies. Those lies will be the death of many. And I am powerless against it." She bent her head to his neck. "But before they do, before they take us all in their wave of sin and fire, I want you here and now, this truest thing we are."

They were the words he'd waited for. His mouth moved to her breast. He would savor her and this time while they had it. Hannah threw back her head and moaned as if exulting in prayer as he suckled.

He could not keep from touching her. When she made sounds of pleasure, he knew that no matter what the rational part of him realized, it was right. They were right together, and nothing could change that.

His own pants were unbuckled in a moment.

He pulled her to the ground in the ash and raised her skirts.

"Join with me," she begged from beneath him.

"Are you certain?"

Boldly, she took him in hand. Overcome, Nicholas punched a fist into the earth. "Hannah, you bring me to the edge."

"Let us go over."

With her fingers, she guided him. She was wet, ready to receive him, and he found his place within her with great care. Hannah closed her eyes and breathed big at his entrance.

"Yes," she whispered. Then, again, much louder. "Yes."

Mayhaps a bit of a demon rested inside every man, good and bad. Charged with a carnal rush he had never know the likes of before, Nicholas began to move upon her. He thrust fast and hard. The salt of her skin and the earthy smell of her, free and sweet, surrounded him as their bodies moved together on the scorched earth.

Like Adam and Eve in Eden, two bodies of everyday lovers instead of two people seeking to ward off the dangers around them, flesh to flesh.

Someone kicked over the candle. It gave a hiss as it went out.

Nicholas brought his fingers between them to play with her secret place. Hannah arched and gasped, each sound in the night another quickening pulse of his heart.

They could only steal these few moments.

For Nicholas knew they were both in danger.

He knew it as he touched her breast. He knew as he brought his tongue to it. He knew it as she came off the ground and over him to rest over his thighs and began to move, when he touched her with a hand that had been in the dirt and soiled her sweet bare skin, and with their bodies joined and the moon visible over her shoulder through the trees above he understood the danger would only grow, and grow, and...

Hannah found her pleasure on him, moaning to the heavens.

He pulled from her before he released his seed. Neither of them needed the complication of a child. Everything was complicated enough.

They lay, clinging to each other, in the aftermath. Whether it was a happy silence, a peaceful one, or a regretful one, Nicholas could not have said. An owl swooped above and hooted as Nicholas rested his head against her breast.

Wind crossed the trees in a light ripple. At some point, the rain stopped.

"What have we done?" Hannah wondered.

"Do you regret it?"

"I will never regret it."

Rising, they separated in total quiet and began the walk home. Hannah retied her waistcoat and, after Nicholas found her coif from among the grass, unbraided her hair in order to braid it again. "Your hair is lovely," he said. "Was your husband fair? I ask because Sally is so fair."

"Charles was dark as night." Hannah stopped walking. "You should know that Sally is not my daughter by birth, nor my husband's."

"What do you mean?"

"We found her, Charles and I. By the pond. She was no more than a day old, nearly dead of cold the poor thing. By God's grace, we were walking that day and I was collecting dandelion. No one had any idea where she came from, so we agreed we would keep her." She said it so easily.

"Someone just left a baby to die?"

She gave one small nod. "I don't like to think about what would have happened to her."

His belief in Hannah's iron will strengthened. "She is a clever young woman." He held out a hand to help her around a fallen tree.

"She is my greatest joy. It is not something I talk openly about, but it is no secret."

"Does Sally know?"

"Yes, though she believes herself to be a changeling."

Nicholas laughed. "That's old magic."

"Just because something is old does not mean it is dead. It was Rebecca who showed me how to mother her with the aid of a wet nurse. I had no time to prepare, nothing a baby needed, and then I had this child. Rebecca taught me all I know." Hannah ran a hand over her face and blinked a few times as if coming awake. "I cannot believe we have dallied while she will hang."

"There is nothing more we could have done tonight," Nicholas said.

"And we cannot do this ever again," she answered.

He hated to hear it, though he knew it to be true. "I know."

"There is no world for us to be together."

"I know that, too."

Sad, separate, they steeled themselves as they briskly walked the rest of the way home. Inside the house, Nicholas locked the door and the two lovers looked at one another. Both were dirty.

"Leave your soiled garments here and I will wash them in the morning." They began to remove the dirtied clothing. Nicholas helped Hannah from her waistcoat.

"I mustn't allow myself to fall apart," Hannah whispered. "I must trust in God. I must believe this will come out right."

Nicholas touched her face. "I hope you are right." But he knew in his bones she wasn't, and it wouldn't. "Good night, Hannah."

"Good night, Nicholas." How he would have loved to fall asleep next to her.

For a long moment he stood in the kitchen, listening to the rain begin to fall again against the walls and windows.

The day had risen and fallen and a man's heart could barely handle it all. If there was an answer to any of these troubles, he could not find it in ink and paper. Instead, he found it in his pocket. The charm Hannah had made him.

He fell into a restless sleep with the charm clutched in his fist.

Chapter Ten

Who could remember the weather, or the clothes one wore, on a day such as the day Rebecca Nurse and four other women were hanged? Being midsummer it was likely hot, but in the years to come Hannah would not remember any of it when she looked back. She would not remember how she got there, to the spot where she stood to watch.

All she would remember were the gallows and the rocks and trees.

Five women, Sarah Good, Sarah Wilds, Susannah Martin, Elizabeth Howe, and Rebecca, were hauled from a wagon up to the wooden platform with their skirts tied around their ankles. They all had to hobble and hop. Rebecca was so frail she barely made it. It had been seven days since her death warrant had been signed and her reprieve reversed, but there was no more the Nurse family could do for her.

Hannah's stomach twisted, but she could not stop watching.

Maybe there would be a miracle.

No. There would be no more miracles. Hannah would stand there and bear witness. She would remember it and write it down best she could, and help Nicholas in writing it better, and she would speak the truth of it to history so it would not be frittered away into myth and legend, worn smooth down like a rock on the shore.

Witches or not, this was a grave injustice.

Reverend Nicholas Noyes stood before the women and spoke of their sentences. "Admit your sin, Sarah Good! You are a witch and it is high time you admitted as such."

Sarah wore dirty rags and her hair hung in loose clumps. "You are a liar. I am no more a witch than you are a wizard! And if you take away my life, God will give you blood to drink."

Her powerful words, a shrill curse from a woman in her last moments of life, carried across the crowd and silenced anything that was still making noise. Maybe they were meant to carry all the way back to her daughter. Dorothy was not present, as the poor child was still in jail.

Hoods were placed on the women's heads.

Sheriff Corwin edged Sarah Good from the platform, and she was silent.

"Mother," Sally gasped in horror.

"Look away," Hannah pulled her daughter to her before the other four women followed suit and Sally carried those memories forever.

Sarah Wilds. Susannah Martin. Elizabeth Howe. Rebecca Nurse.

Five hooded bodies swung, forever silenced.

Hannah would not look away as Noyes spoke to each of the women in turn as he had to Sarah Good. At the moment Rebecca's feet left the platform, her final step, Hannah had forced herself to watch, had clutched for something to avoid screaming aloud. It was Nicholas' hand she found. Whatever he was, heathen or not, she did not care. He, too, thought it wrong.

Hannah took it all in for one more long moment.

Then she walked away before she had to watch Rebecca be cut down.

Before, there had been a crack in Hannah's faith.

Now there was a ravine.

Each of the hanged was a person, and had lived a person's life. Each of them had laughed and cried, probably loved and been loved, lost and ached. She remembered the kind quietness of Rebecca's voice, and her soft worn hands, hands that had held more babies than she possessed

168

fingers and that had stirred a lifetime of pots. All the women had lived lives in their own way and circumstances. Sarah Good had loved her daughter. Sarah Wilds' son was the town constable. Susannah Martin was said to be a hardworking woman. Elizabeth's Howe's husband was blind, yet he visited her often in jail.

So many lives and pieces of lives had ended on those rocks in the past months and yet there still had been no absolute proof of witches. The words of children did not constitute enough to take a life, to take this many lives.

Nicholas was right. This was sensational.

This was also not God's will. It could not be.

As long as the Court of Oyer and Terminer worked unchecked, drunk on their absolute power, it would continue. As long as the girls were believed so utterly completely, it would continue. More souls that didn't deserve it would be stricken from the earth.

Only Nicholas could stop it. He had the Governor's ear.

To save her world, he would have to leave her.

He found her down the road toward home after she stopped because she could not hold back tears another moment. Seeing no one around, he pulled her aside into the tall crops and held her against him as she ranted. "If they hang Rebecca Nurse, they would hang God himself. And they will bury her not in the churchyard. Never was a woman more true to God than Rebecca." Hannah clutched his arm, buried her face in it. "You must write this all. Tell the truth. It is madness. The Devil has taken hold of Salem, and it is not the accused women who work for him."

"Hush," he quieted her lest someone overhear them.

Hannah could not quiet. She wailed from the bottom of her broken heart.

He held her head to his chest and smoothed her hair. "Hannah, you must pull yourself together until we are home again."

"It is not your home," she whispered.

Nicholas did not answer. He brought her up to her feet and held her arms. "You must make it home unnoticed. You must do this, Hannah."

Walking side by side, not touching though Hannah was so aware of him she felt every movement and breath, they made it home.

Sally had gone off somewhere. Hannah knew what the girl had seen and how it would haunt her nightmares for years. Perhaps Sally would have been luckier to be a changeling and escape this ugly world. Later, when she returned, Hannah thought she might hold the poor child close until they fell asleep together, as they had not done in years.

Nicholas managed to make Hannah go to bed. He did not know if she would sleep. He heard movement at times, but she did not emerge. At least she was safe in her room. The cat went with her. He hoped it was some comfort.

In his own room, he found his flask and took the last of the rum.

Hannah's words stuck with him.

This is not your home.

It wasn't his home. If he were to grab his things and run away, no one could blame him. He had been there for the end of the tragic story of Rebecca Nurse, and had done all that he could to better things. There were times when a man seemed to fight stone walls, and this was one of those times.

Thinking of the women's bodies buried right there beneath where they'd died sickened him.

Knowing that Rebecca Nurse would not be buried in the cemetery, due to her excommunication, saddened him even more, despite his lack of a personal faith.

There came a light knock on the door.

"Bittner," Nicholas said when he answered it. "Can I help you? It is late."

Anson wore dark clothes and held a lantern. He looked into the room and then at Nicholas. "Is Hannah awake?"

Nicholas indicated her door. "I don't know. She has not come out."

Anson nodded. "I am going to town. Come with me."

Anson's words weren't actually a request. It was a demand tossed up in the guise of a request, and it was near midnight by then, but Nicholas knew enough to go with it. He grabbed his own dark coat and followed the man out the door and in the direction of Salem Town. Anson didn't speak. Nicholas did not push. They stopped at the edge of a road, just atop a crest of a small hill.

Anson set down his lantern and stuffed his hands in his pockets. "Keep watch with me, son."

"Where are we?"

"Edge of John Proctor's land."

That seemed to be all he needed to know. Time passed while Nicholas questioned internally what was happening. Nicholas noticed the way a few people who lives in houses on the outskirts of town exited their homes and looked left and right before proceeding on. They moved out into the darkness and disappeared like spirits.

Granted, this was a town on edge, but even for Salem this was suspicious. Most people stuck to home at night for fear of what they might encounter.

"How long will you be staying in town?" Anson asked.

"In truth, I don't know. Hannah wants me to return to Boston and speak to the Governor." A heavy sigh came from Nicholas.

"The man I met when you arrived in town carried himself like he knew all the secrets of the universe. You're different now, Cleary."

Nicholas watched a man come from the darkness and rush to meet up with others doing similar before they moved off. "I believe in reason and science. I've never put much stock in religion. In the Enlightenment…"

"Blast your Enlightenment."

"This place could use an age of reason."

"Fine. Use your reason and explain all this, then."

"It could be as simple as disputes over land. Or playacting. Or perhaps a poisoning. Something in the food that causes hallucinations that would lead to…"

"Then why are not more of us affected?" Anson slapped the idea away.

Nicholas kicked the dirt. "I don't know! And it's bloody infuriating."

Anson peered into the dark for a long quiet moment. He didn't move and did not even appear to breathe. He was watching something Nicholas could not see. When the old man spoke, it was barely above a whisper. "See now, the difference between us is that I know there are things I cannot hope to know. 'Tis a great big world, my boy. Man cannot hope to know everything."

"I have to agree with you now."

"Best watch yourself with Hannah. If you get close, people will wonder. She's not one who lets people close to her—it might seem as if she's…"

"Bewitched me."

"I'd hate to see her hurt. She's a good woman and doesn't deserve to wind up on those gallows. No one does. Not even the strange ones. I'd hate to see it happen to Hannah." The words were underlined by not a threat, but a promise.

"As would I."

"You're a good man, Nicholas. A shame you had to come here. I'd leave if I were you. No report you can write will help."

He feared those words were true. It was time to leave Salem. He was no use here. "What in the...," Nicholas stood straight up and pointed at a strange sight.

Three men dressed in black moved across the field carrying something large together and walking in haste. As quickly as they came from the dark, they disappeared back into it. The moon was helpful in hiding them.

Nicholas tasted bile from a fear he did not understand. "What have we been doing out here tonight, Bittner?"

After the men vanished from sight, Anson put a hand on Nicholas' shoulder. "Righting wrongs. Go home now, son."

He walked back to Hannah's in the moonlight.

It did feel like home, this small house in this ridiculous town. A faint light in the kitchen showed him that Hannah was awake, likely working at her hearth. Perhaps the plants would calm her. He knew how the house would smell, how it would look. And he could not hold himself back from going inside.

Hannah stood by the window. "Where've you been?"

"With Anson." He explained as best he could what had happened.

"They moved her," Hannah said quickly. "The Nurse family. They dug Rebecca up from that shamble of a grave. They'll put her in the family plot before sunrise and no one will know. Likely the other families as well. That's good at least."

"What?"

"It has happened to almost every woman hanged. Families reclaim the ones they love."

God, but that was a horrible thought. To dig up your loved ones.

"Nicholas..."

"Do not tell me…"

Hannah pointed to his trunk, which he had left in his room but now sat near the door. "I've packed your things. Ride to Boston tonight. Now. You have influence. Use it and stop any more of this. John Proctor is no angel but he doesn't deserve to die, nor does his wife. Nor does Martha Corey and…oh gods, Sarah Cloyce." Hannah clasped her hands together in front of her like in prayer. "The horror of it all."

"But that would mean leaving you."

"I am no one."

"You are everything. I don't want to leave you."

"And I don't want you to, but this is what it must be. I am but one woman, and not currently at any risk. I am not even a footnote in this story. You can save lives, Nicholas. We didn't save Rebecca, but there are others. We may have been foolish and distracted when we could have been of more use. We cannot be selfish now."

He touched her hair. To think of her unprotected, in this festering sea of demons. "You will be safe?"

"As anyone can be." She embraced him warmly, resting her cheek against his lapel. "I did not ever expect you to stay."

"Hannah…."

The arms that held him held tight. "I don't need you to stay. If my life has taught me anything, it's that moments carry more weight than years. The moments we had were enough for a lifetime. Go and do your best, Nicholas. Take the brown mare in the barn. And know I will not forget you."

"Nor I you." Nicholas looked her right in the eyes, trying to memorize the flickers of amber in her irises. He could tell from the red how hard she'd cried. For that, he would go. He bent to open his trunk and shoved only a few things into his satchel. "I cannot take my trunk on horseback."

"I will send it to you."

"I'll send word, and return your horse."

"I will also tell Sally you said goodbye."

"I will return."

"You may not."

Nicholas touched her cheek, not wanting to admit that even though only fifteen miles separated Salem and Boston, the distance could be a canyon. He did not know what would happen to either of them in the days to come. "For what it's worth, being with you was the closest I've ever been to God."

After one final kiss, which he let linger as long as he could, he picked up his bag and went to Hannah's barn.

In the morning, word spread that the hasty grave of the executed women had been disturbed. But as quickly as the word spread, it went quiet. These secrets would keep.

By morning, Nicholas was in Boston and went immediately to his room to fall upon the bed, asleep. He would see the Governor at first light, and would figure out some way to give the account of what he'd seen to Governor Phips himself and determined to save the town he detested and the people he would never understand. There was blight on Salem Village and outside help was needed urgently.

So Nicholas was far away from Salem Village when men arrived to collect Hannah, for she had been accused.

Chapter Eleven

With the cool night air around her, Hannah watched until there was nothing of Nicholas left to watch, and then locked her door against the outside world and the demons that flew there.

All her skin felt alive. Something was coming.

Hannah clutched her charm pouch to her nose and inhaled the basil.

She lit a candle. Waited.

Come it did, not two hours later.

Reverend Parris, Judge Samuel Sewall, Reverend Noyes, Sheriff Corwin, and a few other armed men stood outside her door with a wagon and torches. Hannah set her jaw. She had been waiting for this moment longer than she cared to remember, possibly longer than even she had realized. At last it had happened.

She had been named as a witch.

It couldn't be helped. She opened the door to meet them.

"Hannah Hibbard, you have been…."

"Aye. I know," she said. She would not fight or resist, but would behave as well as she could and give them every chance to make fools of themselves in her arrest. There would be no stories of her screaming and pleading for the men assembled to carry to their neighbors.

"Mother!" Sally rushed out to join the scene.

Hannah felt her peaceful expression crack. If she could have kept Sally from the fear that showed on the girl's face, she would have done anything. Yet she kept an even tone as she took the girl in her arms, kissed her forehead, and looked directly into her eyes. Speaking so quietly the men could not hear, Hannah urged. "Go immediately and tell Anson what has happened. No matter what, you stay safe. If you think they will accuse you, run to town and get on a boat. There is some money in a wooden box beneath my bed. You take it and go and do not think on me."

"Mother…."

"I am not your mother."

The words were true. Maybe they could keep Sally from winding up like Dorothy Good.

Sally's face hardened, and she seemed to age five years. "Yes you are. And I'll save you."

"Sally!" The girl was already running off in the direction of Anson's. She was fast on her feet and swift of mind. Hannah had to believe those traits would keep her safe.

Who had accused Hannah was not explained, nor was how there had come to be a warrant for her arrest without any examination or questioning. She was loaded into a wagon all by herself and hauled to the Salem Town jail.

Miles later, she was tossed into the darkness of a cell like a bag of potatoes, and Hannah's knees hit the floor hard. It was a wretched place. The stench, the smell of filth and bodies, and the lack of light gave the illusion of a black pit one would never escape from. For a moment Hannah could not even tell if she was alone until she heard their breathing.

There were others.

In the darkness, she could not make out who they were. That was good, for that meant they could not see her. In her head was a list of names and any of them could be right there, the person who brushed against her leg or the cough from the other side of the space. Hannah faltered, and put her hand over her mouth to hold back the sob that rose as she scurried to the bit of window she could see.

The metal bars over the window were cold. They were caged like animals. As if it could do any good, she pulled on the bar. Of course, it did not move. If the bars could be pulled out, someone would have done it by now. She almost dropped to her knees to pray but for the bit of fresh air staying pressed to the window provided.

Would praying do any good? She may not have been a perfect Puritan, but she was not a bad person. She might know plants and the moon, but she was not a witch. This darkness and filth was what a lifetime of following man's rules for obedience to God had gotten her. Had gotten any of them, for the longer she stood in the darkness the clearer it became and the more the bodies around her took shape. Hannah was very much not alone.

"Figured you'd have been in here much before this," spoke a man's voice.

"Who's there?"

"No one of consequence, Hannah."

"Mr. Burroughs?"

The words were true. Maybe it was George Burroughs that spoke them. What difference would knowing who was in the jail with her make? If she was being honest, Hannah knew it was only by a miracle that she had not been jailed before this. She had held on in her freedom as long as a person could. Tears came when she thought of Sally seeing her upon the gallows as they'd seen Rebecca and the others.

"Oh, hush now." Another voice, that of a woman, said from somewhere down around her feet. "You could stay here for months. They might not even hang you. Dorothy hasn't been hanged, nor Tituba."

"Where is Tituba?"

"Boston jail. She's too valuable to keep here."

Hannah wished she could speak to Tituba. Better than anyone, had understood the game being played. By confessing to an untruth, Tituba had saved her own life from people who would not hesitate to put her at the end of a rope. Many thought that to confess to witchcraft when one was not a witch made her less a woman, but Hannah understood. If the world thought something of you and there was no point in arguing it, why not agree to it if it could keep you alive?

Life was so precious. Be it a man or woman, young or old, black or white or Indian, Puritan or of another faith or no faith at all.

"Rest now, Hannah. Get the sleep you can."

The comfort of strangers was all she had now.

Hannah pressed her forehead to the bars of the window and breathed in the little fresh air she could find before sliding down the wall to come to rest with her back against the bricks.

Sally had gone to get Anson. They knew where she was.

Her thoughts went to Nicholas, who had gone back to Boston.

She felt a profound sadness that he did not know where she was, and might not ever know what had become of her if she was hanged.

Stumbling from his bed, and surprised to be in Boston and not in the room in Hannah's house, Nicholas wasted no time. After changing clothes, he began the walk to the Governor's office. With its crowded streets and large buildings and different fashions, Boston suddenly felt foreign to Nicholas. Hannah had said it must be like living on the moon. Indeed, it felt that strange to him now. He passed bookstores and bakeries and cigar shops and pubs, things that once meant the world to him. Now they seemed decadent and foolish and he barely registered them.

Blessedly he was admitted without delay to the office of the Governor and pointed to a seat by a young clerk. Every man waiting in the chairs around him was clean and polished like men who had never touched dirt before in their lives. He no longer envied the gold buttons. Nicholas badly needed to bathe, and realized he should have eaten something that morning.

A few hours passed before he was seen.

Governor William Phips sat behind a majestic carved desk covered with papers and surrounded by maps of Massachusetts, England, and the entirety of the mapped New World. Before his appointment to the position, Phips had been a sea captain. Apparently, if a man discovered hundreds of thousands of British pounds at the bottom of the sea, it meant he deserved to govern a territory. Now the man had a war against the French and the Indians to handle, and the circles under his eyes showed how much effort it was taking.

"Cleary, you look like you've come from hell," the man said without rising.

"I feel it sir. I've ridden all night here from Salem Village."

"Ah, so you have indeed been to hell." Phips groaned as he rose, crossing the room to a mirror and adjusting his fine-trimmed red waistcoat. "A letter would have sufficed."

"With respect, sir, it would not. Apparently my letters have not reached you as of yet."

"I have received all your letters."

Nicholas swallowed. "Yesterday, five women were hanged for witchcraft." From the way Phips reacted, or rather his lack of reaction, Nicholas realized he already knew. "And at least one of them was absolutely not a witch."

"The Nurse woman."

"Yes."

"The Court found her guilty."

"After first finding her innocent. Then Stoughton stepped in and changed their minds. I watched it happen with mine own eyes. There is mountain upon mountain of evidence that Rebecca Nurse was absolutely not a witch."

"Well, she is dead now, so it is no longer a matter of discussion." The words came cold from the Governor, who barely looked up from his papers.

"Now, her unjust death is on your hands. You granted her a reprieve, then turned around and signed the warrant, sir." He added the *sir* with more of a sneering tone than he'd planned, but which he very much meant.

Phips held up a hand. The thick eyebrows above his stern eyes furrowed. "Tread carefully, Cleary."

"There is no time for it. People are dying and will continue to die."

"The Court has been assembled and their word is law."

"What if the law is wrong?"

Phips straightened his collar. "I think you have spent too long in Salem. You return quarrelsome."

At some point, Nicholas had clenched his fists together so hard his fingers were tingling. The callous way Phips spoke of citizens under his leadership rubbed him the wrong way. Was it because they were mostly poor farmers that their fates concerned him so little? Had the Court been appointed merely for the sake of an image?

"So five women were executed, you said. What of the other four. Were they witches?"

No man could answer that question. "I don't know. Do witches even exist?"

"I put a question to you. In the scheme of all things, is one innocent woman's blood worth four witches?" Phips returned to his desk and picked up some papers. "The world is imperfect, Cleary. Hard decisions must be made. If I am wrong, I will live with the stain."

It was heartless. Nicholas released his hands and moved toward the desk. "You haven't been there. It's madness. A child points at a woman she has never met and screams and the woman is accused and tried and hanged based on nothing more than that word."

"It was my decision to allow spectral evidence."

"Spectral evidence is, pardon my words, absolute horseshit. Even Cotton Mather agrees."

He'd stepped in it now. No one had higher authority than the father and son duo Cotton and Increase Mather did with their opinions. To add to it, Phips was close with Increase Mather. It was foolish to bring them into the conversation.

Phips did not look up, but he did suck in a breath.

"You should get a good meal and some sleep, Cleary. Take a bath and a whore. Return to me in a few days when you've recovered your senses. I would be willing to speak with you then."

Nicholas knew he should walk away. He'd stepped over an invisible line and Phips was granting him his very last chance, to save himself.

Without his assignment, he would have no employment, and with an unhappy word from Phips, the last shreds of his reputation would vanish. Nicholas knew his career in Boston was over. Strangely, he felt fine. "I fear how much more horror can happen in a day's time."

Nicholas had never been one to credit put much stock in faith. He'd never thought of anything as a miracle in his entire life.

But at that moment, as if as sign sent from something higher, a clerk entered the room. Carrying a paper, he did not delay in striding directly to Phips to hand them over. "Another warrant, sir."

Phips half-glanced at it before dropping the paper on his desk. "Fine. Thank you."

Nicholas swallowed. The citizens of Salem were no longer just names. "Who?"

"Another witch. They are like ants when you kick over a log."

How long had Nicholas been gone? Not even a day, and more names had been added to the endless list of the accused. When he had first embarked on his mission, they had been just that. Names. Now they were people and faces and he could not contain his outburst. "What is the name?"

"Cleary...."

"What is the name, sir?"

Phips slid the paper over to him.

Nicholas read the dreadful words.

A warrant for the arrest of Hannah Hibbard....

Nicholas wished he had the balls to lift the ornate desk and throw it out the window and shatter the glass. Knowing that was not the way to help Hannah in the moment, he tried reason. "Sir, I know the widow Hibbard. She is whom I have boarded with this past month. There is no way she is a witch."

"She has been named," Phips said as if it was settled. "There in those pages are the explanation and evidence."

"But there are only a few scribbled lines here and it is indecipherable!"

"It is not for me to decide if..."

"Hannah Hibbard is no more a witch than your own wife."

"Cleary!"

But Nicholas was on his feet now and knew he would not sit again, nor would be keep quiet. "You must put a stop to this. The whole madness is an infection. It spreads from one to the next without reason or care. You may think it's far from you, contained up there in those poor farmers. But it does not care about your money or power. You best hope it doesn't catch you." Finished with more than the discussion, Nicholas turned his back on the Governor.

"You walk out of here and your employment is terminated!"

Nicholas put a hand on the doorknob. "Go to hell, sir."

"I am not finished speaking to you," the Governor, his employer, called.

"But I am finished talking to you."

Bleary-eyed, exhausted, and more scared than he had ever felt in all the years of his life, Nicholas hurried to the livery where he had left Hannah's horse. He had never even learned the beast's name. The brown mare had been drinking from a trough but raised its noble head at Nicholas' touch.

"Listen, friend, I hate to ask this of you…"

Not twenty minutes later, Nicholas was racing out of Boston, headed north and hopeful that blasted bureaucracy would allow him needed time.

She had always warned him this could happen, and he had assured her it wouldn't.

Hannah had called it all a sickness without even understanding the full truth of her words. Salem Village was rotten to the very marrow. The next life it would take would be hers unless Nicholas, somehow, did something.

How on earth could he save her from this? He had no idea how, but he had to.

It was Hannah.

Hannah, who laughed. Hannah, who helped. Hannah, who ran in the darkness to the woods and valued the dirt beneath her fingers and feet. Hannah, who was a good mother and citizen and kind to everyone around her. The woman who challenged him and the one who had, by her own magic, made him better than he had been before he'd met her.

Hannah, whom he loved. And whom he had not said as much to.

Chapter Twelve

An entire day passed. Hannah did not leave the cell. She sat on the floor, barely moving, and if she had gotten any sleep it was in fits and starts. Despite how many people were crowded there, and there were so many the jail had run out of shackles, the cell was fearsome quiet broken only when a man would appear at the bars to speak to one of the prisoners. They were given hard bread and stale water two times, but Hannah could not partake of even a sip with the way her stomach turned. Everything smelled of sweat and filth and there was no place for one to relieve themselves in private. Even that bit of dignity had been stripped away from the accused.

Thus far, the accused had been someone else to Hannah.

Now, she was one of them.

Though there were several people in the jail with her that she knew, she spoke to no one. The spirit was gone from the bunch. Elizabeth Proctor sat, pregnant, in a corner of the room and pulled one string from her dress slowly out, and then wrapped it around her finger. Martha Corey coughed and coughed, lying on a crooked bench. Deliverance and Abigail Hobbs paced and muttered to each other. Hannah could not fathom how those who had been imprisoned for months could handle it. No wonder Sarah Good had looked as terrible as she did. Hannah had only been in the cell one day and already wanted to scream and rage, to tear her clothes and beat her head against the bars. Anything to escape, to breathe clean air again and stop sweltering in the filth.

A group of men arrived at the bars at the first light of the next day.

They had come only for Hannah. She had slept but an hour and could barely understand what was being said.

Under the light of torches, the other imprisoned people tried to intercede on her behalf. There was a strange fellowship among the suffering. A few voices were raised, but were immediately threatened back with clubs and shouts.

"This is wrong. It's too quick!" someone yelled.

Something was wrong. Hannah had faced no judges.

As she was only one very thirsty and tired woman; she did not fight. The men bound her hands to take her up the stairs out of the prison and loaded her into the back of a wagon. A bale of hay sat inside, and Hannah took great gasps of fresh morning air as she settled onto it.

They were taking her to the gallows.

They could not be.

It was too quick. It was wrong. Whatever was happening was not like the others, and it was going to happen before dawn to hide the unlawfulness.

When the others had hanged, there had been large crowds. Now as the wagon rolled up to the ledge, Hannah saw only a few men there. The light from their torches put shadows on their faces.

Only one single rope looped over the large branch.

Hannah swallowed hard. She did not move from her seat.

Reverend Noyes was already there, as was Judge Samuel Sewall.

Salem Village was not such a big place that things could happen without the knowing of neighbors. More people began to arrive. Hannah was able to make out faces and voices, and took a moment's comfort when she saw Francis Nurse and some of his family.

Anson charged to the front of the crowd.

"Hannah!"

"Anson!"

"What is the meaning of this?"

Noyes waved a hand. Two guards opened the wagon and came inside to get Hannah. She did not fight, but she did not help them. She let her legs buckle, knowing they would have to drag her. Hot tears fell on her cheeks, and her coif was pulled roughly so it dangled from her hair.

Noyes stood before the platform. "Hannah Hibbard, you have been found guilty of witchcraft."

"She has not been tried!" The small group lurched forward.

Loudly, Noyes aimed his words at Hannah and ignored the calls. "She was seen fornicating in the woods with a devil all in black."

So that was it.

Hannah sought one particular face in particular in the crowd. Only money and influence could lead to a disgrace like this.

At the very front of the crowd stood Harmon Webb, and he did not appear at all disturbed by the goings on. Though she could never have

197

proved it and would never have a chance to try, she knew he had fingers stuck in this pie. He held a torch of his own, and she could clearly see the smirk on his face.

Noyes continued, "Do you deny the charges?"

Hannah shook her head. She would not lie. "I do not deny it."

Whispers in the crowd answered her words.

"And she practices plant medicine." Harmon yelled over the growing roar of the crowd. His charge brought more people in the divided crowd to his side. The side that thought her guilty of enough evil to be hanged.

"Plant medicine does not make me a witch."

The crowd's fury rose. Hannah closed her eyes with the intention to pray.

It was her mother's face she saw when she closed her eyes. Her brave mother, who had hidden herself to be safe. Hannah had done her best to lace up her stays and follow her example, but the rope being slipped around her neck was evidence that it had not worked. Hannah had lived as good a life as she could, and she was still about to die for the crime of simply being different.

She could no longer pray.

"By the authority granted by the court, you will face the sentence of death by hanging."

As if watching it happen to someone else, Hannah felt herself moved up to the edge of platform from which the others had hanged. When she turned to see who was moving her, she saw the face of George Corwin, Sheriff of Essex County. When Charles had passed, the Sheriff had been so kind to Hannah and Sally.

"Mr. Corwin..."

He did not answer her. It was if he didn't know her, didn't even see her.

"Do you have any final words?"

There were a million words she wanted to scream. For every woman through all the years who had not fit the role expected of her and drowned or burned or hanged, for every injustice ever allowed. There were not enough words, and even if there Hannah was not good at them. Nicholas could have spun the words into something. But he was not here.

Movement by the trees caught her eye.

It was Sally. Sweet innocent Sally, who should not see such horrors.

Hannah's heart stopped beating.

Hannah could not go desperate and screaming. Sally would remember her in her final moments. She would be strong and brave and return to the earth. Perhaps she would be reborn as a flower, or perhaps as a tall tree with wide-reaching branches that would give shelter and shade to Sally as grew into a woman, and to the children she would have.

Hannah nearly choked at the realization she would not know her grandchildren.

For Sally, she had to be brave. Remembering Rebecca's bravery, Sarah Good's bravery, Bridget Bishop's bravery, and that of all the others who had stood in this place before her, Hannah set her eyes upon Reverend Noyes.

May he remember her face. "God knows my truth. I don't owe it to you."

"Blasphemer!" and "Trollop!" and others curses came at her, spat by faces she had always known. Also there were words of support and prayers for all the good they did. Anson watched carefully. Sally's eyes had never been bigger.

The last thing Hannah saw was her worn shoes.

They had once been her mother's shoes.

"Mother…" she whispered.

If she had truly been the kind of witch they wanted her to be, she would have burned them all.

The fear in Nicholas' belly grew as he reached Salem Village at nightfall and saw the pond. There was no movement at the Hibbard house and no smoke from the chimney. Sally was not in the garden and the door was wide open. He tied the horse to the garden fence and stormed inside.

The hearth was cold. The embers had gone out. The house was cold as it had never been before. Dough sat in an uncovered bowl. Hannah's knife lay by some dried herbs, and a charm pouch lay in the middle of the floor.

Nicholas fell to his knees and picked it up.

They had already come for her.

His whole coming to the Village was probably pointless. What could one man do against the wall of authority that the Church and the Government made? He had accomplished nothing thus far, and what hope did he have of helping now?

The cat meowed at him.

Turning, he saw Carrot sitting in the doorway staring at him.

"I know," he said in response. "I have to do something. But what?"

Carrot walked outside. Nicholas followed. There were wagon tracks in the dirt outside. He began to follow them, hoping they would lead him where he needed to be.

"Cleary!"

Anson was coming from his house to the road to meet him. Two of Anson's sons, men in their twenties and thirties, were on his heels.

"I was with the Governor when the warrant was delivered. Anson, it makes no sense. And where is Sally?"

"Sally is fine. She stayed with us last night, though she has run off again. They came for Hannah the night before last. It is an underhanded business. There was no examination, no word of the arrest until after it was done. And no trial."

"Mrs. Hibbard is now in jail," one of Anson's sons said.

Nicholas threw back his head. With Hannah in jail, he would not even be able to speak to her. "Who did it? Stoughton? Parris?"

"It was Corwin and Noyes who came for her," Anson said. The old man walked up to Nicholas. "Come inside and eat something. Rest a little too. You'll not do her a lick of good if you faint away."

"How can I rest and eat when Hannah is in danger?"

"Same as anyone around here has done anything while the ones they loved were in danger. And I know you do love her, son."

There was no point in racing to Salem only to scream at the doors of the jail.

"I…will go to the Hibbard house. I will rest there and I will eat something. And I will help Sally as she needs. And I will figure out what is to be done."

When he sat at Hannah's table a short while later, having brought some bread and cheese and ale with him, he felt utterly lost. This was how so many in the community had felt with their loved ones accused. Like they were waiting for someone who might never return.

He kept hoping Hannah would walk in the door. She never did.

Carrot came in, and out, a few times.

Sally returned at one point when the sun had gone down, and upon seeing him rushed to him and threw her arms around him, letting go a torn sob that hit Nicholas deep in his heart. "There, there," he comforted. "I would never have gone if I had known this was to happen."

Sally pulled away, wiped her nose on her sleeve, and shook her head. Through red-rimmed eyes, she looked up at him and kept on shaking her head. "This is the Devil's work, it is."

"Sally," he insisted. "This is the work of bad men."

Shaking her head over and over, she backed away from him. As if she wanted to say something, she opened her mouth. But before words came, she shook her head again one last time and went back outside. He looked after her, but she had vanished into the tall grass.

Nicholas ate without tasting and fell asleep at the table, woken only by a loud banging just as the sky began to change colors with the sun's rise.

"Cleary! They're going to the gallows!"

It sounded like one of Anson's sons. Nicholas bolted up from a hard sleep and ran out the door as fast as he could to the gallows. Lungs aching, legs hurting, he reached town and saw a group of people going that same way.

A gathered group in Salem was never good.

A woman whose face was hidden by a bag stood on the ledge.

Only a few faces looked familiar to Nicholas. Anson and his sons, Sewall and Corwin of course. Then he saw Sally with her back against a tree, and on the other side of the crowd, Harmon Webb looked incredibly smug.

It had to be Hannah on the platform.

"Are you certain you will not confess?" Noyes shouted.

The woman did not answer.

"I will hear your confession," Noyes said. Nicholas heard a tremble in his voice. As if this was somehow wrong and he was stalling. That was interesting. Noyes had been known to taunt the women on the ledge. This was different.

It was almost as if this had not been sanctioned by the court.

Nicholas saw the woman's hands tighten into fists. They were Hannah's hands. He burst into the crowd. "What is going on here?"

All eyes turned on Nicholas. "This woman is accused of witchcraft," Sewall replied.

Nicholas tried to be rational and not hysterical in his response. "But I left town not even two days ago and she had not been accused. That is not long enough for an examination and testmonies and a trial to have happened."

"There was no trial," Anson agreed.

"I have special decree from the Governor." Noyes offered it to him.

Nicholas slapped it away. It was meaningless paper. "Fuck the Governor."

Oh, if they hadn't thought him a demon before they certainly did now. Voices were raised and the ire of the townspeople began to turn from the gallows toward him. There'd be no staying in Salem even if he had wanted to. Not that he would consider it a moment more. Nicholas charged forward, but found himself facing a guard with a musket. "Stop there, sir."

"Hannah!"

"Nicholas?"

The executioner moved as if to push her, and Nicholas figured he could rush to catch her if she swung. He could catch her feet and boost her and it would take the pressure off her neck. He would likely be shot, but could push through. It would be horrible, but she could live. Perhaps. If a miracle happened…

Miracles were ridiculous nonsense.

But then one came. A real one. And it did not come from God.

A scream unlike any scream Nicholas had ever heard came from the crowd.

When he turned, he realized the great big sound was coming from a girl with white hair. Sally stood straight as an arrow, hands clutched to the sides of her face with fingers curved like talons, and screamed a scream of blood and murder to the heavens. The sound could have shattered glass and scared away birds. Yet in her Puritan clothes, she looked like a worldly angel.

Nicholas made a move for the distraught girl, but Sally did not need his help. She pointed one furious finger and all her fury at Harmon Webb.

"It is not my mother who is a witch, 'tis you! Harmon Webb!"

"What is this?" A rumpled Reverend Hale now stood next to Nicholas.

"'Tis your specter that has tormented me. I have seen you outside my window at night!" Sally thrust a hand into the air. "You have aimed to seduce my mother, and have tried to take me away! You have bloodied hands! You are a wizard like the rest! It is you they danced with in the woods!"

The performance was masterful. Of course a few other people in the crowd agreed and began to point at Harmon just the same as Sally pointed. The panic spread, and came immediately to the man's face. "I am not a wizard, Sally."

Sally did not stop pointing. "You lie! You are the Devil in black!"

"I am a full covenanted member of the church."

"So was Rebecca Nurse," Nicholas answered, twisting the knife.

"I have seen you outside my window!" Sally screamed.

Harmon read the crowd, saw the faces turning against him, and swallowed. "I am not a wizard, Sally, but I am your father. I make that confession here and now before God and these men. And as such I expect you to heed me."

At that moment, as he slowly edged his way closer and closer to Hannah, Nicholas felt stupid for not seeing it earlier. Harmon's hair was graying a bit, but he was as fair as Sally. They shared other features, too. Blue eyes, lean frame and long limbs.

How long had Sally known, the clever girl? Did Hannah know?

Nicholas could have applauded Sally's manipulative and marvelous performance. It was so sincere-sounding he wondered if she'd truly believed Harmon to be a specter all this time. He would make sure to clarify that he Harmon was a terrible man but no sort of actual demon as soon as Hannah was off the gallows and much more than one step away from death.

Hannah stood still, skirts and hands bound. The Sheriff had his hands on her arms, waiting for the order from Noyes. Noyes stuttered, trying to stave off the fight that had grown beyond his authority.

"It is true," Anson cried. "Harmon wants Hannah's land and lusts for her. He has wanted her land since Charles died. Don't you see?"

"I would not enter into this," Harmon threatened the older man.

"Or what?" Nicholas shouted. "You will accuse him, too. Will you accuse everyone who calls out your bad actions and evil behavior? Is that the way of things in Salem Village now? But why am I not surprised; it has worked thus far for Reverend Parris and the Putnams, accuse anyone who stands in the way of what you want and blame it on the Devil?"

"That man is not of God!"

"Who was Sally's real mother? I would wager my life 'twas not your dear departed wife, God rest her soul." Nicholas glared at Harmon. "Was it a serving girl? Did you lure her to dance in the woods?"

To reclaim the narrative, Harmon pointed at Hannah. "She was seen in the woods collecting plants."

"You are farmers by and large. Do you fear plants now?"

"The child is a changeling!" Harmon cried.

"Sally is no changeling." But she is marvelous, Nicholas thought. "You, her father, should know that better than anyone. It was you who left her by the river, presumably to die. Why? To cover for your sins? But this woman," Nicholas pointed at Hannah. "This brave and kind woman and her blessed husband took her in and raised her as her own. That is the most Godly act I can think of."

Enraged, Harmon growled like a bear and lunged for Nicholas.

"Cleary!" Hale called in warning.

"Forgive me, father," Nicholas said. The good Reverend John Hale simply averted his eyes and, therefore, did not actually witness the moment when Nicholas punched Harmon to the ground.

"Enough," Noyes called. He waved a hand.

Corwin pushed Hannah off the ledge.

Time stopped.

Nicholas was too far away. It stabbed him in the heart. This was the end. The woman would die. Nothing he had done would mean anything. Quickly he looked for Sally in the hopes that she was not seeing this. Hale grabbed the girl to shield her eyes at least.

It was the most terrible moment of Nicholas' life. He ran for Hannah, hard.

Hannah's body twitched for a moment. Her legs kicked and she swung wildly.

Then something snapped.

Hannah fell to the ground in a hard heap.

Absolute bloody chaos erupted. Sally wrenched herself from Hale and leapt toward Hannah, pushing everyone in her way aside and continuing to scream down the sky. One of the men in the crowd pulled Noyes away, and a young member of the Nurse family Nicholas vaguely remembered conked the executioner so he fell to the ground and seemed only too happy to do it. Rocks were thrown, clothes were torn, and people screamed and scrambled. Judge Sewall tore at his hair.

The sunrise was a beautiful orange.

Nicholas dove to Hannah and pulled the cloth bag off her face.

A line of horrible red circled her neck where the rope choked, and her eyes, also red, seemed ready to pop from her face.

Hannah gasped and winced and folded in half, yet she was alive.

"The rope…" Nicholas unloosed it best he could.

Anson appeared and cut the ropes from Hannah's neck and her hands and feet quickly. Then he stuck the knife in his belt and pulled down the shirt to cover it. "Best go quick. She'll be up here again by noon if you don't leave," Anson urged.

"Was that a miracle, Bittner?"

"Naw, I cut the rope before they strung it up. Got word something bad was happening."

The true miracles were people. "Will you go to jail?"

"Not if no one knows I done it. Get gone. Take my horses if you need them."

"We're leaving," Nicholas urged. "Hannah?"

Managing to clutch his arm but not yet making words, she nodded. Gently, but without hesitation, Nicholas lifted Hannah from the ground. Sally embraced Anson and he kissed her forehead.

"Thank you, Bittner," Nicholas said.

"Go," Anson answered. The old man got lost in the crowd.

"I'm glad you came back," Sally said to Nicholas.

"Good thing I did. I wasn't gone a day and look how much trouble you got in."

"I know a way home where we will not be seen. Come."

Hannah rested her face against his neck, and Nicholas and Sally rushed home as quickly as they could, practically unnoticed by the chaotic scene as it fizzled out like a fire left unattended. Sally took him a way through tall grass that hid them, and allowed them to vanish like spirits.

Chapter Thirteen

For a moment after her feet had left the platform and there had been nothing beneath them, Hannah would have sworn she felt the soul leave her body. Despite the bag over her face, a bright light had blinded her and, somehow, she had escaped the harsh pain of the rope tightening around her neck. It had felt like a hundred years, though likely only a minute passed in total.

She heard her mother's voice, telling her about the plants.

Then the pain had returned. Searing. Throbbing.

There had been more as she'd hit the ground. Never had Hannah hurt as badly or as completely as she now felt, with Nicholas carrying her across the fields. He held her as kindly as he could, but understandably did not slow his pace, and with each step her bones felt and bruised. There was a wetness on her face, and she figured it was blood. It could also have been tears.

Perhaps she fainted, for she woke up at home to find herself lying on the table while Sally rushed to pack important items like the family bible, the box with Hannah's money in it, and some of the herbs and tinctures from the shelves, into a satchel. Charles' satchel.

Hannah remembered what she had heard on the gallows.

This remarkable girl, her daughter regardless of blood, had saved her life.

"Mother!" Sally ran to apply yarrow to Hannah's neck. The medicine stung all the abrasions. "I am sorry about the pain."

Hannah touched her daughter's hand while Sally wrapped a cloth around her neck. Speaking hurt, but she could not keep quiet. "You are wonderful."

Red eyes blinked back tears. "I thought you would die."

"We have to leave. I am sorry."

Sally sniffled and wiped her eyes with her sleeve. "It is only father's grave I will be sorry to leave."

"Harmon Webb is your true father," Hannah said.

"No he isn't," Sally said. "Regardless of blood. Harmon Webb is a bad man."

215

"How long have you known?"

Sally shrugged, almost bouncing from nerves. "The other girls told stories about a woman who worked for him, and then she went inside one day and no one ever sat her again. Abigail Williams mentioned she'd heard there was a baby. I have Mr. Webb's same coloring and not yours and Father's."

It all made such sense now. Perhaps Harmon had wanted Sally as well as Hannah and the Hibbard land. The room spun again.

"Nicholas has gone to get Anson's horses," Sally said. "He's taking Carrot over there, too." She sniffled a bit. "He will be alright at Anson's, I think."

"I think Anson will give him all the love and cream he desires."

"Will Nicholas take us to Boston? Will we live there?"

Hannah fainted before she could answer the question. In her dreams, she saw the faces of the accused circling her, guarding her. When she woke again, it was Nicholas leaning over her.

"I hate to ask this, but can you ride?"

"I will do what I need to," Hannah whispered.

"It will hurt you."

"I do not doubt it."

That he stood before her was the answer to a prayer. Nicholas Cleary had not been the man she'd imagined and desired, but he was the man who had come and who now she could not imagine desiring anymore more than. His strong arms helped her up off the table and out the door.

Hannah reached out one hand and touched the wooden door that had sheltered her for all these years. A swell of sadness rushed over her, and more tears came. They were foolish tears. They had no choice but to leave. After all, it was only a house.

Charles had built the house. Leaving Salem meant leaving him and his grave. Yet, she felt deep in her heart that he would tell her to go and not be foolish. Hannah would carry his memory, and so would Sally. The girl now wore a jacket, with her true father's bag over her shoulder and another on her lap, and sat atop a white horse with such confidence. Charles had taught her how to ride every bit as well as any boy could.

Nicholas swung his own bag over his back and helped Hannah up onto the saddle.

To watch her home fall away as the horses started out hurt something fierce. She would never see it again. There was no other way.

Something had spared Hannah.

Though admittedly her life was spared because of the acts of three very important people— Nicholas, Sally, and dear Anson Bittner—there must have been a piece of God in it.

For all the pain and fear, Hannah still believed.

What she was leaving was an old way of thought. There were new ways of doing things now. All over the world, people found different ways to feel a holy spirit and she would do the same. Injustice had broken her own skin, pierced her ignorance, and now she understood why Nicholas could not help but find himself involved.

Sally looked back constantly. "We are not being followed," Nicholas said. "You can rest, Sally. We will be in Boston in a few hours. We'll send the horses back to Anson and lay low. It's easy to do in a city like Boston. We'll go immediately to my rooms, and then we'll get what we need and decide where to go from there. And I know people, though I will warn you they are not Puritans."

"They will be just fine," Hannah replied.

"Boston," Sally breathed with wide-eyes.

"You were very brave," Nicholas said to the girl. "I was impressed."

"I watched the girls do it so many times," Sally began. "Though I did not like to lie, it was easier than I expected."

"There are moments for breaking the rules," Hannah said. Sweet Sally would have quite an awakening out in the world beyond Salem. She would have liked to say some reassuring words, but with Nicholas' arms around her, she could not fight her body's instinct to fall back into rest.

Hannah dozed against Nicholas for much of the ride. He relished the weight of her against him and the ability to hold her openly in the daylight. They rode beneath the suns warmth, Nicholas made certain to check back often that they had not been followed, and the four hours passed quicker than he had expected.

One could never predict which road they would head down.

Nicholas had gone to Salem Village selfishly determined to restore his own glory and was now arriving back in Boston with a family in tow. A Puritan family, of all things. But Sally and Hannah were his family now, and the thought warmed him.

Hannah had woken. She yawned. "I am a witch, you know."

"Of course. Therefore, I should have let you hang."

"I no longer think things are as certain as I used to. I am a witch, as perhaps some of the others really are. A white witch, a kitchen witch, who does no harm, but that did not matter in the end." When she reached to pull out the last bit of her braid, her rich copper hair fell loose and free over Nicholas' arm.

Nicholas pressed his lips to her hair. "Those still to come will remember Salem Village and these events," he said. "Parris and the others could burn all the papers of the events, but it will not be forgotten. Stories will be told over and over. The stain will remain on families, and grandsons will disavow their grandfathers."

"You really think so?"

"It's the way of the world, Hannah. Bad things happen, usually helped along by men who think they have the best of intentions, and then those same men think they can erase it. But stains like the madness in Salem Village cannot be washed away." Seeing the way tears came to her cheeks, he put his lips to her forehead again and squeezed her gently. "Do not cry. There will be better times."

A long time passed before she said, "What will we do in Boston?"

It was the only thing Nicholas had considered for the whole of the ride. "We cannot stay in Boston. It is too close to Salem Village, and too likely someone would recognize us. Also, it is possible I may have angered the Governor."

"*May* have?"

"I most certainly angered the Governor. I will not repeat the words I said to him."

"Goodness. Where then?"

"I thought Pennsylvania. At least we could avoid a Massachusetts winter." Hannah's eyes drifted off to the land around them. Hannah was a Puritan woman, and was leaving a place where Puritans were everywhere to go somewhere where other groups she had been raised to see as enemies were flourishing. It would be hard. "The Quakers have their own faith, but they will welcome you. We can buy a piece of land, and can farm, and I can write anywhere. It is a beautiful country with lots of mountains and hills. Giant forests. There may even be new plants for you there."

Hannah rested her hand on his knee. "We will make a life together."

"If you choose."

"I do choose. I choose you. I will find my faith again. I do not need the Salem meetinghouse to do so."

Slipping his head to the side, he set his lips upon hers. For a moment he stayed there. Hannah was really against him, in his arms, alive. "I returned and heard you'd been accused. I thought I'd lost you."

She only nodded. "I believed I was lost. Perhaps you were my salvation."

"Marry me."

"Aye."

"And you, Sally, will you allow me to marry your mother?"

"I'd like that," Sally said, and actually smiled. "Will you teach me more about Joan of Arc?"

Boston came into sight. The rest of the day passed quickly into night as the three tired souls ate hot meat pies from a pub and then fell into a hard but comfortable sleep until the following dawn in Nicholas' room.

At first light, he packed his things, paid off the landlord, sent word to Anson as to where to find his horses, and purchased a small wagon.

Nicholas enlisted a clever dressmaker he knew to quickly find Hannah and Sally some garments that would not immediately brand them as Puritans. He left the women with Francesca, with whom he had once dallied away a summer, and rushed to fill the wagon with supplies for their journey: flour, blankets, apples, some dried beef and fish, a rifle, knives and things for cooking and eating. On an impulse he also purchased a stack of books and paper and more ink.

He had much writing to do.

When he met them again, Sally wore a dress of deep rose. She spun in it and marveled at the floral stitching along the neckline. To see the girl smile made Nicholas feel he had done the right thing to bring them here.

Hannah's dress was the color of plums. Despite the bandage around her neck, now clean and tidy, she stood tall again. Her hair had been twisted back, and those strong and beautiful features shone clear as day.

"How do you feel?"

"I feel a new woman."

Leaving Boston behind, Nicholas peeked at the family beside him and then forward. They were not smiling, and shared a great deal of nerves. Sally rode in the back, already making her way through the new books.

Hannah sat beside Nicholas while he drove the horses. "Are you ready?" she asked.

Nicholas leaned in for a kiss. There, in broad daylight at the edge of a city full of people, he allowed himself to feel her there beside him. When they parted, and Hannah laughed softly and set her head on his shoulder, he urged the horses forward.

There would be no record of Hannah Hibbard or Nicholas Cleary in the story of Salem Village. No one would speak of them or remember them, for they were not of importance in the events.

They vanished, gone like ghosts.

Afterword

All told, twenty five people died due to the Salem Witch Trials. Nineteen by hanging, five died in jail, and Giles Corey was pressed to death. Two dogs were also killed.

The trials came to an end in 1693, at which point the hysteria was fading and public opinion had shifted. When the wife of Governor William Phips was accused, he ordered an end to the trials.

Judge Samuel Sewall was the only judge ever to apologize for his role in the trials. In the years after, he wrote against slavery and the mistreatment of Native Americans, and also in favor of women's rights. He wore a makeshirt hair shirt for the rest of his life to atone for his part in the witchcraft hysteria.

Twenty-five years after Sarah Good stood at the gallows and said to Reverend Nicholas Noyes, *"You are a liar! I am no more a witch than you are a wizard, and if you take away my life God will give you blood to drink,"* Noyes died of a hemorrhage. He literally choked on his own blood.

Author's Note

Not many events in American History have been written about more than the Salem Witch Trials. I have made my very best attempt to get everything right and accurate, but as if often the way with history, sometimes sources say different things.

Many of the original documents from the trials no longer exist. As such, I have taken some liberties. Hannah and Sally Hibbard, Anson Bittner, Nicholas Cleary, Harmon Webb, and James Andrews are fictional characters.

Below is a list of notable sources I consulted in writing this book.

Any errors are absolutely my own fault.

Sources

- *The Witches*, by Stacey Schiff
- *Six Women of Salem*, by Marilynne K. Roach
- *A Storm of Witchcraft: The Salem Trials and the American Experience*, by Emerson W. Baker
- *Witches! The Absolutely True Tale of Disaster in Salem*, by Rosalyn Schanzer
- *Salem Witch Judge: The Life and Repentance of Samuel Sewall*, by Eve LaPlante
- *A Little Commonwealth: Family Life in Plymouth Colony*, by John Putnam Demos
- *Unobscured* (Season One), a podcast by Aaron Mehnke
- The Salem Witch Museum website, https://salemwitchmuseum.com/

The Author

Marie Piper is a graduate of Michigan State University, a former actor/director, and a lover of stories. She's especially interested in writing stories set in the wild history of America.

Marie lives in Chicago with her husband, kiddo, and three cats. In non-pandemic times, she goes on adventures with her zany family, reads everything she can get her hands on, loves visiting all the museums Chicago has to offer, and tweets too much. (The tweets have increased because, you know, pandemic…)

Visit mariepiper.com or find her at @mariepiperbooks for more information.